The
ZEE FiLES

Girl / Friend

The ZEE FILES

Girl / Friend

BY TINA WELLS

with Stephanie Smith
Illustrated by Iliana Galvez

WEST
MARGIN
PRESS

For my nephew, Alexander. —T.W.

Library of Congress Cataloging-in-Publication Data

Names: Wells, Tina, 1980- author. | Smith, Stephanie (Stephanie Danielle), author. |
   Galvez, Iliana, illustrator.
Title: Girl/friend / by Tina Wells with Stephanie Smith ; illustrated by Iliana Galvez.
Description: Berkeley : West Margin Press, 2022. | Series: The Zee files ; book 3 |
   Audience: Ages 9–12. | Audience: Grades 4–6. | Summary: Everyone is surprised
   when Zee strikes up a friendship—and more—with Archie, the school's most elusive,
   handsome boy on campus, but unfortunately Zee's friends and Archie do not get
   along, and the more she tries to help the situation, the more tangled things get.
Identifiers: LCCN 2022000542 (print) | LCCN 2022000543 (ebook) |
   ISBN 9781513209470 (hardback) | ISBN 9781513135021 (ebook)
Subjects: CYAC: Boarding schools--Fiction. | Schools--Fiction. | Dating (Social customs)--
   Fiction. | Friendship--Fiction. | LCGFT: Fiction.
Classification: LCC PZ7.W46846 Gi 2022 (print) | LCC PZ7.W46846 (ebook) |
   DDC [Fic]--dc23
LC record available at https://lccn.loc.gov/2022000542
LC ebook record available at https://lccn.loc.gov/2022000543

Printed in China
25 24 23 22 1 2 3 4 5

Published by West Margin Press®

WEST
MARGIN
PRESS

WestMarginPress.com

WEST MARGIN PRESS
Publishing Director: Jennifer Newens
Marketing Manager: Alice Wertheimer
Project Specialist: Micaela Clark
Editor: Olivia Ngai
Design & Production: Rachel Lopez Metzger

FSC
www.fsc.org
MIX
Paper from
responsible sources
FSC® C102842

1

ZEE'S BIG NEWS

*T*he buzzing of the phone stirred Mackenzie "Zee" Blue Carmichael from a rare eight hours of sleep as she blearily looked at the screen. *Good morning, sleepyhead,* the text message read.

Archie Saint John used to send texts to Zee only in the evenings before lights out. But since they became officially girlfriend and boyfriend, he texted her every morning. First he'd text, *Good morning,* then to ask, *Did you dream about me?* and finally, *Let's get breakfast.* In the beginning, Zee thought the sweet messages were cute. Then she wondered how long and how many messages would keep coming.

With one eye open, Zee tapped out a reply: *Morning. You're up early.* She put the phone back down on her nightstand and turned over for a few more minutes of sleep.

The phone buzzed again a few seconds later. *I woke up thinking about you,* Archie quickly responded. *Shall we get breakfast this morning together?*

Zee sighed. She looked up at the ceiling in her dorm room

at The Hollows Creative Arts Academy, the premier creative arts boarding school in the U.K. Then she turned toward her roommate Jameela Chopra's bed, which was already made with the comforter smoothed out and pillows carefully arranged. Zee thought back to the last time she ate breakfast alone, with her roommate, or with anyone else besides Archie. When was the last time she had a message on her phone that wasn't from Archie? She wondered if she'd ever have a morning to sleep in, to journal and write, to eat whatever she wanted for breakfast and not have an audience of Archie Saint John watching her every move. But now there was little time for daydreaming, because she had to get herself presentable for her fourth breakfast date of the week. Zee tossed back her blanket, got out of bed, and headed for the shower. She let out a big breath. *Being a girlfriend is a full-time job*, she thought.

It had been less than a week since Archie asked Zee to be his girlfriend. She had kept the news under wraps, except for telling her best friends Chloe Lawrence-Johnson, who lived back in California, and Ally Stern, who lived in Paris. Zee couldn't keep anything from them. She had texted the girls the same night Archie kissed her and asked her to be BF/GF, and for the next couple days she had sent a flurry of texts and posted messages to the Zee Files, the private file and messaging system the girls had created to keep in touch with each other across continents and time zones. Zee uploaded pictures and screengrabs of Archie's texts to the file, like a photo of the turmeric latte they always ordered at Moe's Coffee Shop on Main Street. She also uploaded a selfie of Archie and her together in front of the dorm two nights ago. It was their first picture together as a couple.

After returning from the shower, Zee saw Archie had sent two more messages. The last one said: *Meet you at 7:30 for breakfast?*

It was 7:15 a.m.

Yes? Archie followed up when Zee didn't respond immediately.

Yes, she replied, hurrying to get dressed. Zee fixed her hair into a tidy ponytail, the red curly locks cascading down her back, and put on a smear of highlighter on each cheek, just to look a little fresher to meet up with her new boyfriend.

Jameela, looking ready for a full day of classes in her crisply ironed Misha Nonoo uniform jacket, a white button-down shirt, and a navy pleated skirt, walked into their shared bedroom to grab her books for the day. "Morning," she said.

"Good morning," Zee replied.

"Busy day ahead?"

"Class, study group, a little soccer. You?"

"The usual. Class, dance, dinner. I've got to pick up something at the ballet studio before I go to class. Are you heading to breakfast?"

"Yes, but I'm going to have breakfast with Archie."

"Archie, Archie, Archie," Jameela said. "Correct me if I'm wrong, but you seem to be spending a lot of time with Mr. Archie Saint John, is that right?"

Zee pursed her lips. It was impossible to hide the truth about her and Archie any longer. "I guess I hadn't told you yet," Zee said. "Archie and I are boyfriend and girlfriend."

Jameela brought her hand to her chest. Her eyes widened and her mouth dropped. "Excuse me? You and Archie are what now?"

"Yes, Jameela," Zee said, smoothing her hair. "He asked me to be his girlfriend a few days ago. We've been together since."

Jameela looked at Zee, her eyebrows raised. "Like, *together* together?"

"Yes."

"Like, you two have kissed?"

"Yes, nosy-pants, we have kissed."

Jameela rolled her eyes, her eyebrows up toward the ceiling. "Oh. My. Goodness. I can't believe it's happened. But I'm not surprised by the way that you two have been having these private meetups and jam sessions since you arrived on campus."

Zee grabbed her backpack. "Music is something we're both passionate about, yes. But now that you mention it, we haven't worked on any music together since the Festival." The Hollows had just held its annual Creative Arts Festival, the biggest on-campus talent show of the year, and Zee had wowed the crowd with her debut performance.

"Speaking of music," Jameela said, "what does Jasper think about this new relationship?"

Jasper's opinion of her new relationship was one of the reasons Zee tried to keep the news under wraps. Jasper Chapman was Zee's closest guy friend, and she really valued his opinion. They first met when Jasper moved from London to California and attended Brookdale Academy with Zee. The two bonded quickly over their love of music, but then he had to move back home to London after a year. When Zee's family had planned to move to the U.K., her parents enrolled Zee at The Hollows in part because Jasper was already attending there. Jasper was reliable, creative, and welcoming to most people. Except to Archie.

Jasper thought Archie was too standoffish to be a good friend, or anything else, for Zee. "He's just this privileged kid who can practically get away with murder because he has money," Jasper had said on more than one occasion. But Archie opened up to Zee in ways he didn't open up to other people. And that special bond made a solid foundation for a relationship. *At least that's what all the magazines say*, Zee thought.

"I don't know what Jasper thinks," Zee said. "He doesn't know yet."

"He doesn't?" Jameela said, surprised. "Isn't Jasper your best mate?"

"Yes, but you're my roommate and I'm just getting around to telling you."

"True," Jameela said. "This is what happens when I spend all of my time at the dance studio. I miss out on such important things. So does this mean you'll be having all of your meals with Archie now? Should I not wait for you for dinner?"

"No, that's not what it means. I'll still have dinner with you and Jas and Tom. I still have my own life," Zee said.

"I hope so," Jameela said. "I wouldn't want Archie to swoop in and then we never see you anymore."

"Don't worry, that won't happen."

"Right," Jameela said. She grabbed her backpack from the floor near her dresser. "I'm heading out. I definitely want to catch up later and hear more about your *re-LAY-shun-sheep*."

"Don't say it like that," Zee giggled.

"Well, that's what it is, isn't it?"

Zee let out a loud sigh. "I'll see you at dinner."

• • •

Zee made her way across the quad toward the main dining hall where she agreed to meet Archie for breakfast. She usually grabbed something quick at the smaller dining hall in the dorms before rushing off to class, but since her new boyfriend wanted to have a morning meetup, Zee met Archie at the larger dining hall because it was in between their two dorms.

Zee walked inside the building. She spotted Archie sitting alone at the table toward the back, his eyes directly on Zee. She made her way over and put her bag down on the seat across from him. "Good morning," she said.

Archie stood up and reached his hand out for hers. "Hello, sunshine. You look nice. All good?"

"Yes, just fine," Zee replied. "I smell eggs."

"Grab yourself some. I'll put it on my card."

Zee walked ahead of Archie toward the food stations, craving a bit of independence to at least choose the breakfast of her choice, even if he wanted to pay for it. *I can pay for my own breakfast and I do have my own ID card*, she thought. She scooped herself a serving of scrambled eggs, toasted some whole wheat bread, and smeared a pat of butter on the toast. Archie paid for their breakfasts and they sat down at the table. Zee ate quickly. She was hungry and anxious about her first-period algebra class in which there may or may not be a quiz, depending on how her teacher Mr. Stevens was feeling.

"This weekend I'm going away to Scotland," Archie said. "My dad's got some work there and wants me to come. Mum's coming too. She wants us to spend more time together as a family."

"Scotland sounds cool," Zee said, her shoulders lifting at the potential of having some time to herself in the coming days.

"Yeah. But if you're not there, then it won't be as much fun."

Zee shrugged her shoulders. "It's okay. You need to spend more time with your family. And this weekend I need to spend some time here studying."

"I'll try to be back by Sunday so that we can have the night together," Archie said.

Zee shrugged her shoulders again. "Really, don't worry about rushing back. Do your thing. I'm not going anywhere. Not this weekend anyway."

Zee looked at her phone for her schedule for the week. This afternoon she had a study session with Izzy and Jasper she was looking forward to. She hadn't hung out with them outside of classes and meals all week because Archie had taken her out to Moe's Coffee Shop for an after-school snack every day. Zee also had on her schedule a soccer scrimmage this weekend and a possible conference call with Chloe and Ally. Both were dates she was eager to attend.

"Eek, I'm going to be late," Zee said, standing up to take her garbage to the trash and head out for classes.

Archie looked up. "Rushing out already?"

"Archie, we have class in four minutes. I want to get to mine on time."

"All right, Cali, we'll go," Archie said. He slowly stood up from the table while Zee hurriedly took their trays toward the trash bins. She was already near the exit when she turned back and saw Archie checking out his teeth in a mirror hanging next to the register.

"Archie!" she said

"Hold on, I have something in my teeth," he said, not in a rush. He made a few funny movements with his mouth before finally backing away from the mirror and walking toward the exit.

If they delayed any more, Zee was going to miss the first-period bell. As they made their way out of the dining hall and across the quad, she saw Jasper walking ahead of them toward the glass-and-concrete mathematics building where their algebra class was.

Archie called out to her from a few paces behind. "Cali, wait up."

"I can't, I'm going to be late to maths," Zee said. "Let's just catch up after class." She gave Archie a quick kiss on the cheek, then rushed off.

As she turned back to the building, her eyes connected with Jasper's. He turned his back and walked through the door, not waiting for Zee to catch up.

• • •

Zee ran across the quad to the mathematics building, trying to catch up with Jasper before he entered the classroom. She swung the doors open and jogged down the hallway, almost bumping into two upper-level students, and arrived at class just as Jasper took his usual seat in the front.

"In a hurry?" Jasper asked jokingly.

"No," she said, breathlessly. "I just didn't want someone to take my seat."

Jasper looked her up and down. "Uh-huh. No one's taking

your seat, Zee."

"Well... anyway. What's up? Going to study group this afternoon?"

"Yes, of course. Wouldn't miss it," Jasper said.

Just then, a bubbly Izzy Matthews walked in, her blonde hair swinging behind her. "Hey, guys!" she said to the room, her phone in her hand recording her entrance. Izzy filmed her life at The Hollows for her popular YouTube vlog and usually captured footage of her classes before and after the teacher's lectures.

"Hello, everyone! Morning! Good morning! Good morning!" she said in her usual perky tone. She waved excitedly to Jasper. He returned the gesture with a head nod. Zee smiled, tilted her head, and gave a peace sign as Izzy walked by.

"Study group this afternoon?" Izzy asked, pointing her phone camera at Jasper and Zee.

"Yes, indeed!" Jasper said.

"I'll be there," Zee said.

"Great," Izzy said.

As Izzy took a seat in the middle row of class, Jasper leaned over to Zee. "So what was that kiss you gave Archie on the quad? Is that how you usually greet each other? Quite friendly for two people who are just friends. In fact, it's extraordinarily friendly for Archie Saint John."

Zee felt like this was the beginning of a conversation she had been dreading to have with Jasper since Archie asked her to be his girlfriend. But she couldn't hide it anymore.

"Well, not that it's a big deal or anything, but Archie asked me to, um, well, be his girlfriend," Zee said, stumbling over her words. "I mean, we're already friends, you know. And so, yeah, now we're, like, more than friends."

Jasper looked at her blankly. "You're what?"

"You heard me," Zee said.

"You and Archie Saint John?" Jasper said. "Get out."

"Yes, Jas."

"I can't believe it. But maybe I can? I don't know what to say. What do I say? Congratulations? Watch yourself? I really don't know what to say."

"How about say nothing and just be happy for me?"

Jasper looked at her directly. "I can't say that I'm happy for you being the girlfriend of the one person on campus I'm not fond of," he said. "I want to say you should stay far away from Archie. And that he only cares about himself. And that I've seen him be generous to nobody but himself. But if you're happy, then I'm happy. So I guess all I'm saying is just be careful."

"Duly noted," Zee said, taking out her notebook and

textbook. She shook her head, frustrated that Jasper was so against her relationship that was less than a week old.

Izzy looked over from her seat. "What's all the chatter?"

Jasper looked at Zee. "Zee and Archie are together."

"Together? Together doing what?"

"Like, together. Like boyfriend and girlfriend. Like a couple."

"Reeeallllllyyyy?!" Izzy leaned back in her seat and put her hand to her clavicle. "I knew it! I knew this was going to happen! When did this happen? Have you kissed yet?"

"Well, yes, we have kissed," Zee said, feeling heat rise in her cheeks.

"Wow, this is serious! I mean, I never fancied you as Archie's type because he's so posh and whatever, but this makes so much sense. The music thing, and you're the new girl in school. Of *course* he's into the hot new thing. I mean—" Izzy searched for the right words to fill the silence. "Congratulations!"

"Thank you, Izzy."

"Now if you need to go on a date with your boyfriend instead of coming to study group, I'll understand," Izzy teased.

"I'm not going to blow you guys off for Archie!"

"All right, just checking," Izzy said, snickering.

Zee looked over at Jasper. His eyebrows dropped and his lips pursed together as he flipped the cover of his algebra textbook open. He turned away from Zee just as Mr. Stevens entered the room. Zee wanted to say one more thing to Jasper, but she knew whatever she said he would no longer be interested.

"All right," Mr. Stevens said, putting his briefcase on the top of his desk. "Who's ready for a pop quiz?"

2
TWO FRIENDS, ONE ZEE

Zee felt unsettled about neither Jasper nor Izzy being overly supportive about her relationship with Archie. Jasper seemed disappointed. Izzy seemed more eager to watch the soap opera unfold than truly happy that her friend had found a boyfriend. Zee fought to keep her concentration on the handouts during algebra class, and she had no idea how she performed on the pop quiz. She hoped Mr. Stevens would grade on a curve and that the rest of the class had been just as distracted as she felt.

After algebra, Zee headed to sciences with Mr. Roth where she would be with Izzy and Jasper once again. They were studying the oceans for this section of class, and Zee was very interested in each lesson. The latest class assignments were group projects geared toward developing experimental projects, plus fundraisers, to clean garbage from the oceans. During the week Zee had spent her few moments not with Archie researching ideas, both things that she'd seen in recent news reports and old notes from a similar class project back at Brookdale.

At the end of class, Zee hurriedly gathered her books and supplies. She caught up with Jasper just as he walked out of the classroom into the hallway.

"Hey," Zee said, tapping Jasper on the arm. "Listen, I understand your concern about Archie. Yes, he is a loner. Yes, he is a rich kid with money to do whatever he wants. And yes, he has had some troubles. But we do have a lot in common. And he has been very nice to me. And I will protect myself. I'm not completely clueless."

"I understand," Jasper said. "I just want to make sure that you're keeping your eyes wide open. Make sure you don't lose yourself in this... relationship."

"I know, and I won't," Zee said. "Besides, I want us to keep spending time together working on music and things. I had a lot of fun producing that song for the Creative Arts Festival. We should jam more often."

"All right," Jasper said, a smile slowly growing across his face. "Meanwhile, what do you think about this oceans project? Want to work together?"

Jasper and Zee walked down the hall chatting excitedly about their homework. "I found my old notes from Brookdale when I did that Save the Oceans project last year. We can use those to inspire us," Zee said. "Of course it would be helpful if we could go to the ocean at some point to see it. Do you think people here get to see the ocean at all?"

"Of course, Zee," said Jasper. "Mainly during holiday."

As they walked down the stairs of the building, Archie was standing at the bottom, waiting for Zee. He leaned against the railing with his arms crossed. "Cali," Archie called. His mouth was not smiling or frowning. His eyes gave a flat stare.

Zee looked up at Archie, surprised. She wasn't expecting to see him until after lunch and was looking forward to spending her morning break alone. She usually took the time to head back to her dorm and either grab a snack, look over her notes, or send silly texts to Chloe and Ally. Sometimes she simply zoned out and did nothing. Alone.

"Archie!" Zee said. "Have you been here waiting for me?"

"Of course. That's what I do," Archie said slyly.

"I was going to go back to my dorm room to study before my next morning classes."

Archie looked at Jasper. "Jasper," he said.

"Archie," Jasper replied curtly.

Archie looked at Zee, reaching out for her hand. He took a step toward her. Zee looked down at her shoes as he moved in to give her a kiss on the cheek. Jasper's eyebrows raised high onto his forehead. "I guess I'd better run. Zee, I'll see you in Skills for Life," Jasper said.

"Yeah, Jasper, she will, thanks," Archie said sarcastically.

Zee's mouth dropped open. She looked at Jasper. "I *will* see you in Skills. We'll catch up some more there," she said. As Jasper walked away quietly, Zee watched him for a few seconds, annoyed at Archie's tone toward her friend.

"What's with you and that Jasper chap?" Archie asked.

"What's with *you* and that Jasper chap?" Zee snapped back. "Jas and I are good friends. He went to my old school in California and he was the only person I knew at The Hollows when I got here."

"Ah, right," Archie said. "Well, now you know me as well as you've gotten to know Jasper, right?"

"I'm *getting* to know you," Zee replied.

"Right," Archie said. "Shall we head to Moe's?"

"I was going to go back to the dorms to call my mom."

"You can do that at Moe's, right?"

"I'd like a bit of privacy," Zee said. She was eager to speak with her mom as they hadn't chatted longer than a few minutes since the Festival weekend. Zee wanted to see if her father had told her mother anything about Dr. Banks, the school therapist. Zee had asked her dad to keep it a secret that she was seeing a therapist, but she knew she couldn't hide it from her mother forever. She thought today might be the day she drummed up the courage to tell her.

"Okay," Archie said. "Well, let's head back to your dorm then. I can wait for you in the lobby or outside while you make your call."

"By then it will be time for class," Zee said. "Why don't we just meet up later, around lunchtime? Or I'll see you in music theory later."

Archie's face turned serious. "I can't meet around lunchtime because I've gotta meet my rugby mates. We have a game this afternoon and I've gotta pick up some of my gear from them. And we can't really talk in music theory. Why don't we grab a quick latte now and then we'll make it back before your next round of classes? C'mon."

Reluctantly, Zee slowly turned toward the school's main exit. Archie gave her a smile, put his arm around Zee, and guided her out to the town square.

• • •

Though Archie had a reputation for being standoffish, when he was with Zee he talked nonstop. Ideas, schemes, and stories often flew out of his mouth like a river of random thoughts. He talked a lot about himself, but hardly asked Zee what she was interested in. When he did ask questions, it was to find out what Zee was doing, where she was going, and who she was with. Zee sometimes zoned out when Archie was talking, her mind drifting off to something more interesting, such as who were behind some of the world's greatest inventions, like the laundry machine or the ice cream scooper.

"I thought about creating an app so kids on campus can buy and sell used goods to each other," he said as Zee ordered their golden turmeric lattes. "Sort of like eBay, but specifically for The Hollows students here. I have lots of music equipment and gear at home that I'm trying to get rid of. And I'm sure

other kids around here have old instruments, art supplies, or other stuff they could sell. Like, why not just create this marketplace that could include books or school supplies and whatever?"

What seemed like hours to Zee but was actually ten minutes passed by. She didn't hear much of whatever Archie talked about, and now she needed to head out for her late morning classes. Zee stood up from the table and gathered her personal items in her bag.

"Helloooo," Archie said, "where are you going?"

"It's time to head back to campus," Zee said, looking at her phone. "We've got class in five minutes."

"Oh yeah, right, class," Archie said. *Did he forget that it was the middle of a school day and that school was where two thirteen-year-olds belonged during school days?* Zee wondered. "I'll study in the dorm. I'm not really digging my English class these days. Easier for me to just do the work at home and then turn in homework."

"Suit yourself. But I've gotta go."

"Wait up," Archie said. "I'll walk you to class."

Zee turned away from Archie and rolled her eyes up toward the ceiling. The one thing Zee didn't like to do was to make a ruckus by entering class late. It was bad enough that she was struggling in English lit, but being late and struggling through class was too much of a burden for Zee to handle. "Okay, hurry. I don't want to be late."

"Okay, gotcha, chill."

"Chill? Archie, you're not going to class, but I am."

Archie slowly got up from the table. "All right, you want to leave me, fine, go ahead. I'll see you for lunch."

"Lunch? I thought you had plans?"

"Nah, you're my plans now," he said. "Rugby can wait."

Zee shook her head. *He really needs to find some other people to hang out with,* she thought as she gave him a quick kiss on the cheek and rushed out the door. She took a deep breath then walked as fast as she could toward campus, already feeling less suffocated than she did while sitting in the coffee shop across from her very wordy boyfriend.

3

FOUR PLUS ONE IS... A CROWD

After a full day of classes, Zee checked her cell phone and saw Chloe and Ally had started a group text with her.

Chloe

> So, how goes things with Archie?

Ally

> Yes, details please! Excite me with your tales of love.

Zee wished that she could tell them about her and Archie taking long walks across the quad, looking deeply into each other's eyes. Or dropping love notes on each other's desk during music theory, or writing songs about each other during after-school jam sessions. But Zee had only tales of frustration. She felt smothered. How was she supposed to take time to think and create and write songs when Archie was always... *around*?

Things are great. Archie is sweet. A little overattentive. But that's a good thing?

Um, overattentive? Like your mother?

Kinda?

Like a mom who means well, but she's still all up in your business?

Zee pursed her lips together as she texted back, *Exactly.*

• • •

Zee planned to join Jameela, Jasper, and Jasper's roommate Tom Anand for dinner in the main dining hall. It was the one meal of the day she looked forward to because Archie usually had rugby with his mates until late and Zee could catch up with her buddies. She even wanted to hear about Jameela's ballet practices, even if she knew only a few of the correct terms for the movements.

After a full day of classes and studying, Zee went back to her dorm room and found Jameela getting ready to head to dinner, changing out of her ballet tights and putting on a skirt with her new jacket uniform.

"How was dance? Hashtag *plié all day!*" Zee teased her roommate.

"Funny," Jameela said. "I'm ready. Tom just texted that he's at our usual table already. Let's go."

The roommates walked across the quad together, passing groups of students giggling and catching up on their day. They hustled toward the main dining hall door as the chilly fall air blew steadily across the quad. As they reached the entrance, Izzy appeared right behind them, holding her camera up to film the two walking in. "These small moments matter to my followers," she explained to Zee and Jameela. "Even when we're just going to eat. People love it."

The girls took in the sights of the busy and brightly lit room buzzing with students eating and chatting. Izzy left to find her roommate Poppy as Zee and Jameela walked toward Tom and Jasper, who were already settled at their usual table.

"Hi, guys!" Zee greeted.

"Greetings," Tom said, his beaded bracelets jingling on his arm as he waved. He looked at Jameela and smiled. "How was school and dance?"

"All right on both fronts, thank you," Jameela answered sweetly. Zee looked at her friends. Their demeanor had become warmer toward each other lately compared to what it was at the start of school. Since the Festival, Jameela and Tom showed more concern for each other's schoolwork and arts projects than before.

"I'm going to grab food. Shepherd's pie is the special," Jasper said, quickly walking off. Zee and Jameela put down their things and followed Jasper and Tom to the food stations. Jameela headed for the salad bar and loaded up a plate with all of the greens they had at the buffet—spinach, arugula, alfalfa sprouts, broccoli, and edamame. She topped the greens with some chickpeas, grated parmesan, and a sprinkle of walnuts, added a few slices of cucumber as a garnish, and a drizzle of olive oil made the meal complete. Zee headed back to their table with a veggie burger and sweet potato fries.

"Did you guys do the Skills homework yet?" Jasper asked. Skills for Life was the only class that the whole group had together. Today's lecture had been centered around cakes. "Do we have to bake a cake before tomorrow's lecture?"

"If we have to *eat* a cake as part of our research, I can definitely get the assignment down," Zee joked.

The crew excitedly talked about their favorite cakes as they ate their meals. Zee laughed at all of their jokes, happy to have a silly conversation about cakes with her friends, and her mind drifted. *What if I could write a song about cake? I mean, if Rihanna could do it, so can I. Cake mates, cake dates, sugary sweet between you and me...*

Just then, an unexpected guest sauntered up to the table and plopped his tray down next to Zee's.

"What did I miss?" Archie said, then gave Zee a peck on the cheek. Zee stared in disbelief at Archie. The suffocating feeling in her chest began to swell.

"Hi, Archie," Jameela said.

"Greetings," Tom said.

"Archie," Jasper said.

"Jasper," Archie said.

Zee felt queasier by the second. She thought Archie had rugby practice and would have dinner with his mates. But here he was, right next to her, sitting so close to Zee that his knee brushed up against hers and she could hear him chewing his food. She had not had a meal on her own in two days. "What did I miss?" Archie repeated.

The conversation cooled with Archie's arrival. Everybody went from chatting excitedly about their days to concentrating on their food. Zee tried to add some levity to the moment.

"Archie just came from rugby. Jasper, don't you play rugby?"

"I haven't played rugby since I was seven," Jasper said. "I've been concentrating more on my music production. And a bit of basketball here and there."

Archie ignored this altogether and changed the topic. "Anyone here have Ms. Longsworth's English class? I'm not buying this whole thing about her being a Rhodes Scholar by the way she teaches."

"Nope," Tom responded.

"Why don't you have Mrs. Pender's class like most of year nine?" Jameela asked.

"Because I missed so many days last year," Archie said. "Family obligations. Just finishing up last year's work, and then I'm moving to Mrs. Pender's English class."

An awkward silence crawled across the table. Zee tried to change the subject. "Tom, are you working on any new poetry?" she asked.

Tom nodded. "Actually, Jazzy Jas here is helping me remix a poem into a song."

Zee answered, "Really? I'd love to hear it."

"Well, you can come over any time and listen. Or we can meet up at the music hall and play it for you."

"Great!" Zee said. "How about tomorrow?"

"Cali, we have plans," Archie cut in. The group turned toward Zee and Archie. Zee turned to look at him too.

"We have plans? What plans? You said you were going out of town," she said.

"I'm leaving in the afternoon, but before that we have plans."

"No, before that I have school," Zee said. "What does you leaving have to do with me listening to Jasper's music?"

"We'll talk about it later," Archie said coolly.

The group exchanged confused looks. "Speaking of music, Tom, let's get back to the room," Jasper said. "I just got an idea for a riff for the track."

"I'm going to get another apple for a snack for later," Jameela said. "Zee, should I wait for you?"

"It's okay, I'll meet you back in the room. I won't be long,"

Zee said. Jameela picked up her tray and walked off toward the food stations, while Tom and Jasper grabbed their trays and headed for the exit. Zee seethed at how Archie took over both the dinner conversation and her social calendar.

She turned to Archie. "What was all that about?"

Archie looked at her. "What?"

"Why did you say we have plans when you know you're going away to Scotland for the weekend? You're not even going to be here tomorrow. What does it matter what I do when you're not here?"

"I'm your boyfriend and I don't know if I like the idea of you hanging around other guys when I'm not here."

"Jasper and Tom aren't 'other guys.' They're my friends."

"Let's talk about this later," Archie said dismissively. "I'm leaving tomorrow. Let's enjoy the evening and then we'll meet here back in the morning for breakfast before I go."

"What if I have plans in the morning?" Zee said. "You assume that all of my time is going to be spent with you."

"What better things do you have to do?" Archie asked.

"For one, study," Zee said. "For two, uh, maybe put on a nice face mask? Clean my room? Study with Izzy and Jasper?"

"Or you can take your books and study with me," Archie said.

"But you don't even study half the time! When have we ever studied together?"

"You could study and I can watch you study."

"That doesn't sound like much fun for either of us," Zee said.

"Listen," Archie said in a stern voice. "We are a couple, so we should be spending as much time together as possible."

That suffocating feeling overtook Zee's ability to breathe and think normally. She had to get out of this conversation quickly. "I like hanging out with you, but I don't need to spend every waking moment with you. And you don't need to spend every waking moment with me. Don't you get bored of me?"

"Bored? No," Archie said. "Just looking at your face makes me smile."

"Oh, that's sweet. Really," Zee said. "But sometimes this face needs a facial. Sometimes this face just needs some sleep. Sometimes this face needs to look at something else for a change."

"All right, I get it," Archie said. "Why don't we walk back to your dorm for one last hang before I go?"

Zee looked at him blankly. With those words "one last hang," she knew her face would not see a face mask, or algebra homework, or anyone else besides Archie Saint John this evening. She vowed to herself that she would use his Scotland trip to reclaim her time—and her relationships with people outside of her very clingy boyfriend.

4
TIME FOR A BREAK

*F*riday showed promise of being a wonderful day. The sun was shining. Zee's curls were frizz-free and uniformly coiled, the hallmarks of a good curly hair day. Zee knew there would not be a pop quiz in algebra because Mr. Stevens planned to introduce an entirely new chapter during the lesson. And she knew Archie was leaving for Scotland in the morning, which meant she'd have at least three days all to herself to catch up on homework, hang out with her friends, video chat with Chloe and Ally, and do whatever she wanted.

Zee got dressed for the day, quickly gathering half of her silky curls into a high ponytail. She grabbed her uniform blazer hanging on her desk chair and put it on, and slid her cell phone into the pocket. Jameela got ready at the same time, and the two listened to music on their portable speakers, dancing and giggling as they left their room.

As they walked, Zee's phone buzzed in her uniform jacket, but she was so engrossed in conversation with Jameela that she didn't bother to fish it out to see who it was.

"So what is going on with you and Tom?" Zee asked.

"What do you mean, going on? There's nothing going on!" Jameela said, flustered. Her cheeks turned a deep shade of pink. "He's nice. He's really nice. And means well. But there's nothing going on."

"Uh-huh," Zee said, smiling.

"No!" Jameela said. "I've got school and dance. I don't have time for a boyfriend. You of all people know how time consuming a boyfriend is."

"Yeah, all too well," Zee said.

As the two walked out on the main quad, Zee saw Jasper. "Jas!" Zee called out to him.

Jasper gave a nod and walked toward the girls. "Morning, ladies. What's cracking?"

"You look quite dapper today, Jasper," Jameela said.

"Why, that means a lot coming from you. I'm meeting Mr. Hysworth about my concentration." All students at The Hollows created custom arts concentrations of their own to pursue during their time at the school. "Thought I'd clean up a bit so he didn't think I was slacking," Jasper said.

"Good idea," Zee said. "Hey, got time for a jam session later today? I've got some ideas for songs I've been working on.

"I think the question is, do *you* have the time?" Jasper said.

"What does that mean?" Zee said. "Of *course* I have the time! And if you must know, Archie is out of town for the weekend."

"So that's why you want to hang out with me. Because Archie's not around," Jasper said.

"No, that's not it. I asked you earlier this week if you had time to jam."

"Yes, I remember, I'm just giving you a hard time," Jasper said. "I'm free this afternoon. Let's meet up right after class."

"Great, I'll see you then."

Zee could feel a buzzing in her jacket pocket again. She wondered who kept calling but didn't check the phone. "Let's walk to maths together."

"Yeah, shall we?" Jasper asked.

"I'll see you all later," Jameela said. "Lunch today?"

"Of course," Zee said.

Jasper and Zee walked toward the mathematics building, chatting about the weather, the almost bare trees lining the main walkways, and plans for the holidays coming up. Zee's phone was still buzzing as they entered the classroom and took their seats. Just as she was about to pull it out to see who it was, Mr. Stevens walked into class. "All right, let's get started," he announced. She took out her algebra notes and started scribbling away.

• • •

"I guess we will be working on the lesson during our study session with Izzy today?" Zee asked Jasper as they left class. Mr. Stevens had dismissed them after a long and complicated lecture that left Zee's head spinning.

"Probably," Jasper said. "We may have to turn our jam session into a maths session too."

"Let's not work too hard. There's always time for music."

Jasper chuckled as they made their way toward the building's exit. He held the door open for Zee and followed her through, skipping down the short flight of stairs. At the bottom, a familiar but unhappy face stared up at Zee.

"Cali."

Startled, Zee saw Archie staring back at her. "Hey," she said. "I thought you were leaving for Scotland this morning."

"I am," Archie said, "after my first round of classes. I wanted to see if we could have tea later before I leave. But it seems you're too busy to respond to my texts." Archie spoke with a bitterness in his voice.

Jasper looked at the two together. Archie's face looked hard, like was annoyed that Zee was talking to Jasper. Jasper slowly backed away from the pair and turned toward the sciences building. "I'll see you in class, Zee."

Zee nodded, frowning as Jasper walked off in a hurry. She turned back to Archie, her back straight and chest forward. "I've been busy this morning," Zee said. "I haven't even looked at my phone."

"Well, perhaps you should look at your phone. I've been texting you all morning."

Zee took her phone out of her pocket. The screen lit up with fifteen new texts from Archie. Her eyes glazed through some of them. *Hello. Hi. Hi, Cali. Miss you. Moe's before I leave today? Hello? Anyone home? Cali... CALI! Moe's? Turmeric lattes? You and me?*

Zee looked up. "I'm sorry. I just got caught up this morning. Chatting about school and stuff."

"Chatting," Archie said. "With Jasper."

"Chatting with Jasper and Jameela, my roommate, and Mr. Stevens, my algebra teacher, and other kids in my class. Chatting with people. With students. On this campus. Yes, chatting."

"Right," Archie said, walking closer. "Well, from what I just saw it looks like you're too busy chatting with just Jasper. Maybe you should take a break from him. He's probably told all sorts of bad things about me anyway."

Zee's chest felt heavy and that annoying suffocating feeling returned. "It doesn't matter who I was talking to," she said. "Look, it's nine o'clock in the morning. I don't want to fight. I thought you were gone and I was busy. It's not a crime that I didn't respond to your texts."

Archie's eyebrow furrowed. There was no sign of a smile on his face. "There would be no fight if you just stopped hanging out with that Jasper."

Zee tilted her head to one side and put one hand on her hip. She pointed a finger at Archie. "First of all, I barely see Jasper. Second of all, you can't tell me who I can spend time with. You're not my dad. You're my boyfriend."

"And you're supposed to be my girlfriend, which means you spend all of your time with me."

"Uh, no," Zee said. "I didn't sign up for that. I am your girlfriend because I enjoy whatever time we do spend together. But that doesn't mean *all* of our time should be spent together."

Archie looked perplexed. He shook his head, trying to shake off his disappointment. "Okay, look, why don't we just go to Moe's and talk about things?"

"I can't. I have sciences right now," Zee said. "Don't you have a class too?"

"I thought I'd blow it off because I figured we'd go to Moe's before I leave for Scotland."

"See, why would I blow off my own class to go to Moe's with you? Why would you assume I would do that? This is what I mean by taking all of my time!"

Archie backed away in a huff. "Fine, go to class. Go hang out with Jasper. I'm going to Scotland. Maybe we can catch up when I get back."

"Go to Scotland. Clear your head," Zee said. And then she said the words she knew in her bones needed to be said. "Let's take a little break from each other."

Archie's mouth fell open. He looked down at his shoes and slowly walked away from Zee, nodding his head slowly. "Okay. Goodbye, Cali." he said. He turned his back and walked away.

"Archie," Zee called. He never turned back. Zee sighed heavily, feeling bad she may have hurt Archie's feelings. But she was also relieved about reclaiming her time. Zee turned toward the sciences building and hoped she would make it to class before the school bell rang.

5

EVERYONE HAS AN OPINION

*D*r. Emma Banks sat in her office wearing a vibrant red-and-green blouse, wide-legged black slacks, and a stack of engraved gold bangles, stylish enough to go from her office to brunch with her girlfriends. Her hair was pulled back from her face, which made her skin look even smoother under her office's overhead lights. Dr. Banks's face relaxed into a smile when she saw Zee come through the door and sit in the chair across from her desk. Her legal pad was already turned to a blank page.

"Hi, Zee," Dr. Banks said, her greeting warm and comforting like a fresh loaf of bread. "It's so good to see you. I can't wait to hear what's been going on these days."

"Things are good," Zee said. "Some things better than others."

"That's good to hear. It seems you got a very warm response at the Festival."

"Oh yeah!" Zee said excitedly. She could hardly get the words out fast enough. "I've gotten tons of people asking me to perform with them or at parties and things," Zee said. "I'm working on new music, which is exciting, and I'm working on some things with Jasper too! He's such a great producer."

"Yes, he is great. He's very talented," Dr. Banks said. "And how is school? Classes going all right?"

"Classes are classes, really. Maths are maths, sciences are sciences. Our oceans project is coming up. We're supposed to study devices designed to clean up the ocean and then try to come up with our own ideas."

"Sounds right up your alley, yes?"

"Yeah. I'm all about saving the earth."

"Great. And what else? Anything troubling you this week?"

Zee's mind drifted to Archie. She wanted to be honest with Dr. Banks about her relationship with him. She hadn't revealed much about him before, but her frustrations with Archie were affecting her overall happiness.

"Yes, there is. I told you about my friend Archie, right?"

"Yes, you mentioned him a few times."

Zee took a deep breath. "Well, we have become boyfriend and girlfriend, but I had no idea how much work it was going to be."

"I see. When did this happen?"

"Right after the Festival."

"And how is it going?"

"It's kind of stressful," Zee admitted. "He expects me to spend every waking hour with him. He texts me in the morning first thing, at night, and after every class period. And he shows up after each break expecting me to have every meal with him. I feel like I have no personal time. Like, I have things I need to do too."

"Indeed," Dr. Banks replied. "Those types of relationships

are intense and should be entered by two people who are very mature. It's extremely different from just being friends with someone."

"Well, I'm mature," said Zee. "But I'm also, like, busy."

"Of course," Dr. Banks said. "Then you need to set expectations with him. Just because you're in a relationship doesn't mean that all of your time needs to go to him."

"I tried to tell him that," Zee explained. "But it didn't end well."

"What do you mean?"

"I tried to tell him that we needed more space, and he basically stormed off across the quad and we haven't spoken since."

"Hmm," Dr. Banks said. "If he's reacting that awfully when you simply expressed concern about your time, that probably shows how he values it."

Dr. Banks placed her legal pad on her desk and leaned in toward her patient. "Zee, you've got so much going on right now. You're adjusting to a new school. You're making new friends. You just performed at the biggest talent show on campus. Why don't you give yourself some time to find your own place at The Hollows before you get into a relationship?"

Dr. Banks sounded more like a big sister and less like a therapist. "I'm sure Archie is nice and everything," she continued, "but there's no need to tie yourself to one person, especially since you've only been here for a few months."

Zee nodded her head. "I guess I was just excited. I like spending time with him. I just didn't know what his expectations of a girlfriend were. I actually had to Google 'girlfriend' to see what I was supposed to do," she said.

Dr. Banks let out a chuckle. "If you have to Google it, it's probably a sign that maybe you should take your time before getting into a relationship."

Zee shrugged her shoulders. She thought she was a little in over her head with Archie. But she didn't want to stop hanging out with him completely.

Dr. Banks said to Zee, "Why not try being friends with Archie and see what happens? From friendship is where true, deeper relationships develop."

Zee thought about what she might say to Archie and what his reaction would be. What if he got mad? What if he never spoke to her again? "I don't know," Zee said. "I hope he'll be okay with it."

"What's more important is what *you're* okay with," Dr. Banks said. "And it doesn't seem like you're okay with how things are now."

Zee took a deep breath. Things had moved a bit fast with Archie. But they didn't have to end completely—just slow down. Archie could have more time for his rugby buddies. Zee could have more time for her music. And both of them could spend less time texting and have more time for their studies. Besides, they seemed to have more fun when they were just friends. In fact, Zee had more fun with all of her friends— Tom, Jasper, Izzy, and Jameela—than with her boyfriend.

"You're right," Zee said with a nod. "I'll talk to Archie."

• • •

Chloe and Ally's faces took up Zee's entire computer screen during their conference call, which Zee scheduled for Saturday evening. Chloe munched on popcorn as if she were watching a riveting documentary. Ally rested her head on her hand, similar to the way Dr. Banks did when Zee talked during their weekly sessions.

Zee spoke rapidly as she recounted the events between her and Archie. "Then I realized, 'I just can't.' He was trying to dictate every single moment of my day. I mean, I couldn't even use the bathroom without having to tell him what I was doing or expecting him to show up in the bathroom stall. I liked the attention, but it was a little ridiculous."

"That would annoy me," Chloe said. "There are some things I just don't want my boyfriend to see me doing. Like eating marshmallow fluff."

"What is marshmallow fluff?" Ally asked.

"You know that fluffy melted marshmallow in a jar that you use to make Rice Krispies treats? It's so good but really so bad for you. I don't want anybody else ever to see me eat the stuff. It's basically melted sugar. But it's delicious."

"I've never tried it," Zee said. "Do I need to?"

"It's gooey and gets everywhere and sticks all over your fingers and face, and it's just like a mess. So yes, absolutely!"

"Sounds like fun," Zee said. "Anyway, I told him I needed a break."

Chloe and Ally made the I-just-drank-unsweetened-lemonade squinty face at the same time.

"Mmm, yeah, so you basically broke up," Ally said.

"No, I didn't say that," Zee replied. "I just need some space."

Chloe and Ally made the same sour face again.

"Space!" Chloe said. "Bye, Archie!"

"No, I don't mean permanent space! Just enough space for me to hear my own thoughts for a minute. Space, like, maybe we should go back to being just friends."

"Whoa!" Chloe's eyes grew as big as dinner plates. "What did Archie say?"

"I haven't told him the friends part yet."

"Oh. So what did he say about the 'break' part?"

"He said, 'Goodbye.'"

"Goodbye, like, for the weekend, or goodbye, like, forever?"

Zee thought about it for a second. "I honestly don't know."

Chloe and Ally looked blankly at Zee. "Mmmmmm."

"Yeah. I know. But the good news is at least I'll have a whole weekend to do whatever I want and not have to worry about text messages or meeting up or doing my hair or wearing date clothes."

"That's true," Chloe said. "You should go out and buy some marshmallow fluff just to celebrate your newfound freedom."

"Well, I'm not going to go *too* crazy," Zee said. "That stuff just sounds gross!"

6

MIXED FEELINGS

*Z*ee felt that her weekend by herself was time well spent. She got a good amount of studying in—she researched and organized notes for her science project, reviewed her English lit lectures, and finished her algebra homework. She wrote song lyrics in her journal—some of them were about Archie, but most of them were about her friends and things that she was inspired by on campus, like birds and spiced hot chocolate, and the first frost over the quad.

She also explored new parts of the campus that she hadn't spent much time on before, like the courtyard tucked in the center of the library hall, and the pond near the south end of campus. Zee never realized how beautiful it was, especially with the birds fluttering over the water. *It's the little things you notice when you have time to yourself,* Zee thought.

On Sunday morning, Zee, Tom, and Jameela grabbed turmeric lattes at Moe's Coffee Shop and brainstormed ideas for their culinary dishes for the final project of their Skills for Life class—a Sunday roast cooked by and shared with the entire class. By dinnertime, Zee realized she had not heard from Archie all weekend. She figured he had returned to campus by now so he could unpack and be ready for Monday's classes. She checked her e-mails for any notes from her boyfriend (*We're still together, right?* Zee wondered), but there were none. He hadn't even sent her a DM on Instagram. Zee opened the photo album on her phone and browsed through photos of her and Archie together. She couldn't help but smile at his chiseled features and green eyes. Zee sighed, then fired off a quick text:

Zee

> **Hey there, have you made it back yet?**

An hour went by with no response. She sent another message:

Zee

> **Well, hope you make it back safely. Can we catch up when you return?**

Another hour went by. Zee became engrossed in her algebra homework, reruns of *The Great British Bake Off*, and hearing about Jameela's upcoming dance recital. At 10:45 p.m., she was ready to tuck into bed before she realized she had not heard from Archie all night. Perhaps he was taking this space thing seriously.

• • •

On Monday, Zee woke up earlier than usual. Part of her was anxious about the week's schoolwork, but she was also nervous about what would happen with Archie. She checked her cell phone to see if she had any new text messages. There were no notifications.

Zee rose out of bed and began to get dressed. She decided that she was going to spend most of the day concentrating solely on her studies and not worry about Archie. She grabbed a quick bowl of cereal and an apple in the dorm cafeteria, and walked toward the hall where assembly took place every Monday. She found Izzy, Tom, Jameela, and Jasper sitting near the front and took a seat next to Tom. She looked around for Archie, but didn't see him among the sea of uniformed students. But right before Headmaster Smythe took the mic, her phone vibrated.

Archie

I made it back. Miss me?

Zee

Of course. I'm sorry.

Archie

Meet later under our favorite tree?

Zee

Sure.

• • •

Zee walked over to the big oak tree on the east side of the quad, where students sat to eat their lunch, study, or enjoy some downtime in between classes. Zee and Archie sometimes met there after class before grabbing lattes or to hang out. Zee took a seat on the bench underneath the tree and waited nervously. Five minutes went by before she spotted Archie walking across the quad toward her. Zee bit her lower lip nervously, and when he got closer her heart fluttered. She really did enjoy being his girlfriend. But she also needed some time to think.

Archie kept his hands in his pockets as he approached her. "Cali. Had a good weekend?"

"Yeah," Zee said softly. "How about you?"

"Good. Scotland was great. Family was okay." Archie waited for a beat then looked out the corner of his eye at her. "I missed you."

"I missed you," Zee said back. "Listen, I feel bad about what happened the other day."

"Me too," said Archie.

"I just wanted to clear up some things that I said before you left."

"Like when you said you didn't want to spend any more time with me?"

"That's not what I said, and that's not what I meant," Zee said. "Maybe we should tell each other how much time we actually want to spend with each other."

"Any time that I have, I want to spend with you," Archie said.

"And any *free* time I have, I want to spend with you."

"Define 'free,'" said Archie. "Is 'free' any time you're not with Jasper?

"Why is this all about Jasper?" Zee asked.

"It's not all about Jasper," Archie said. "But he does seem to be the only person I'm competing for your time with."

"I don't spend all of my free time with Jasper!" Zee said. She was tired of Archie's possessiveness. Dr. Banks's advice sounded in her mind.

"Okay, I have an idea," Zee said. "It seems that we want the same things. We both want to spend time together. Great. But we're not, like, expressing ourselves clearly."

"Seems like," Archie said.

"Right," Zee continued. "Why don't we say what we want at the same time, and then from there we can try to explain what we each mean. Does that make sense?"

"Not really," said Archie, "but I'll try it, just for you."

"Great," Zee said. She stood in front of him, their faces just a foot from each other. "Ready? One... two... three..."

The two blurted out their true feelings for each other at the same time.

"Let's be together!" Archie said.

"Let's be friends!" Zee said.

An awkward silence fell between them. *Oh no,* Zee thought. *This won't end well.*

Archie slowly started to back away from Zee. Zee's mouth tried to form words, any words, but nothing came out. Finally, Archie spoke. "Okay."

"I'm... but..." Zee said.

"Friends," Archie said, backing away even faster. "I don't have many friends, Zee. I'm not good at being friends. But if it's what you want, it's what you want."

"Archie," Zee said. "I still care about you. I still want to spend time with you. I just..."

"Right," Archie said, then turned and walked away.

"Archie," Zee called to him. But it didn't stop him from leaving Zee and walking toward his dorm. Zee bit her lower lip, disappointed at herself for hurting her friend. She took a seat under the large oak tree, looked up at the sky peeking through the bare branches, and watched for any sign in the clouds of what to expect from the next phase of her relationship with Archie Saint John.

THE DOCTOR SAYS

*T*hough the Carmichaels were both aware of Zee's struggles
at school, Mr. Carmichael had told his wife that he would
handle things with Zee. It had been his idea for Zee to visit a
therapist after a few of her teachers wrote home noting Zee's
aloofness in class. Zee had agreed to therapy, though she'd
asked her dad not to tell her mother about it for the first few
weeks and he had kept his word. But Mr. Carmichael finally
told his wife shortly after the Creative Arts Festival, where
the family briefly ran into Dr. Banks. Mrs. Carmichael had
been relieved that Zee was getting help. But she was also upset
that she was the last to know Zee was seeing Dr. Banks, and
insisted on a family meeting with the therapist.

For Zee's next appointment, the Carmichaels drove from
Notting Hill to The Hollows campus in the Cotswolds and met
Zee and Dr. Banks in her office.

"Good to see you, doctor," Mr. Carmichael greeted Dr. Banks
when he and Mrs. Carmichael arrived. Zee nervously wringed
her hands.

"Lovely to see you both. Please have a seat," Dr. Banks said, gesturing to the chairs in front of her desk.

Mrs. Carmichael slowly sat down. "Forgive me, but I'm still getting up to speed on all of this. I was just informed a few days ago that my daughter was seeing you. Honestly, I'm a little troubled by that."

Mr. Carmichael piped up. "That's my doing. Zee asked me to keep the visits from you for a little while, so I honored her wishes. She didn't want to worry you."

"Yeah, Mom," Zee said. "I just didn't want to give you something else to worry about."

"I understand, but I'm your mother," Mrs. Carmichael said, looking at Zee. "How could I not know my daughter was seeing a therapist? You should have told me."

"Mrs. Carmichael, I understand where you are coming from," Dr. Banks chimed in. "And I apologize if I played any part in your frustration. I, too, followed Zee's wishes to keep her visits between us during our assessment period. But you are her parent, and you should certainly be aware of what sort of things your child might be bothered by."

"Exactly," Mrs. Carmichael said, leaning back in her seat, and nodded. "And Zee, if you ever have something troubling you, you know you can come to me."

Dr. Banks smiled. "First, I must say I think Zee is a lovely girl. She's extremely creative and talented, and I can tell she's a wonderful addition to The Hollows community."

"Thank you for saying so," Mrs. Carmichael said proudly.

"Now, Zee and I have been meeting for about a month now…"

"A month?" Mrs. Carmichael said, taken aback. "You've been meeting for a month and I didn't know?"

"I told you Zee was going to talk with someone, honey," Mr. Carmichael.

"Yeah, but my daughter goes to a therapist for a month and no one tells me?"

"Honey, I told you when we first got the letters from her teacher I would speak with Zee and take care of it. I told you Zee was going to talk with someone. So, here we are."

Mrs. Carmichael's frustration was impossible to ignore. "I can't believe a stranger knows more about my daughter than I do."

"Mom, she's not a stranger," Zee said. "Not anymore, really."

"Yes, though I'm still not your mother, Zee. But Mrs. Carmichael, there are things she has brought up during our visits that I wanted to discuss with you," Dr. Banks said. "I also conferred with my colleague Dr. Castellan about Zee and he offered his opinion. I think this might give you some insight as to what I think could be troubling Zee."

Dr. Banks flipped through her notes as she spoke. "Zee described being distracted in a few of her classes, and how she often had this feeling that she wanted to escape to someplace else during class. Has Zee ever expressed these feelings to you before?"

"Well, we know she daydreams a lot," Mrs. Carmichael says. "She's always thinking about song lyrics or stories. That's what a singer does, right?"

"Indeed," Dr. Banks said. "But in class, Zee told me she has this unsettled feeling that coincides with feelings of wanting to escape."

Mrs. Carmichael shrugged. "Who wants to be in algebra class anyway?"

"That's what I said," Zee said.

"And I agreed," Dr. Banks said. "But my point is, Zee is feeling quite anxious about her performance in class. It could stem from this sense of alienation or loneliness from being in a new school, in a new community, in a new country, and feeling like a stranger."

"Right, that makes sense," Mr. Carmichael said. "Is that true, honey? It seems you've adjusted well. You have tons of friends, right?"

"Yeah," Zee said. "New friends. Different from Chloe and Ally though."

"But that doesn't mean things don't seem unfamiliar," Dr. Banks added. "Just the fact that her friends or teachers speak with an accent or use words she hasn't heard of may make her feel different from her peers."

"I see," Mr. Carmichael said.

Dr. Banks continued. "I've also noticed that when she tells me stories about things that make her happy or excited, she tells them in this sort of circular manner. They start at a center point and fan out to these other tangents, or branches or facets if you will, and then migrate to other topics. And there's nothing wrong with that—it just shows the type of thinker Zee is, which is helpful in thinking about what type of learning or communication she best responds to."

The Carmichaels nodded their heads as they listened. Dr. Banks leaned toward them, her forearms resting on her desk.

"Have you ever heard of attention deficit hyperactivity disorder?"

"Yes," Mrs. Carmichael said. Mr. Carmichael nodded.

"Wait, that sounds bad," Zee said. "Am I sick?"

"No, not at all," said Dr. Banks. "Are you familiar with anybody who has it, in your family or in daily life?"

"No," Mrs. Carmichael said. "Are you suggesting that Zee has ADHD?"

"I think it could be a possibility," Dr. Banks said. "One thing to know is that it presents itself differently in girls from how it does in boys."

"How so?" Mr. Carmichael asked.

"With girls it can be more subtle, like with the daydreaminess and the inability to concentrate and feel anxiety in certain classes. These things can be managed with a few different approaches."

Mrs. Carmichael nodded her head and looked at Zee. "Is this because I haven't shown her enough attention?"

"No," Dr. Banks said firmly. "Nothing that you've done or

not done would cause this. ADHD is a disorder marked by hyperactivity or impulsive behaviors. And it's rooted more in how she responds to certain situations, rather than anything you've taught or not taught her. A lot of kids also have trouble focusing during certain tasks or conversations."

"So now I have a disorder?" Zee asked.

"What I'm saying is you have some of the same characteristics as other children with ADHD have," Dr. Banks said. "But you also are experiencing anxiety that could be temporarily causing some of these things. Now, Mr. and Mrs. Carmichael, have you ever noticed Zee trail off during conversations or race between thoughts?"

The Carmichaels nodded. "She daydreams at the dinner table," said Mrs. Carmichael. "But that's what most kids her age do, right?"

"Exactly," said Dr. Banks. "But some kids who do that might also have a harder time concentrating in class or in conversations that are more linear. And if Zee knows that about herself, she might be nervous to be in situations like in classrooms or with new people who may not express themselves the same way. So if we can find a way for Zee to streamline her thoughts, ways for her to stay focused on a task at hand, she may manage better in her classes."

Mr. Carmichael leaned in. "What sort of ways are we talking about?"

"Some of the treatments people have considered include a mix of medicines along with therapy..."

Mr. Carmichael popped up. "I do *not* want to medicate my child!"

"I understand," Dr. Banks. "Like I said, some people

have *considered* medication. And many kids have seen improvements with medication. For Zee, given that I've only been seeing her for a short time, I'd like to see her for a few more sessions, then confer with Dr. Castellan about next steps."

"Yes, that's right. Surely our child doesn't need drugs," Mrs. Carmichael said. "What are some other options?"

"We've already started a journaling exercise, which she claims has been working very well for her. Right, Zee?" Zee nodded her head, and Dr. Banks continued. "But there's also certain kinds of brain exercises that we can try as well to help her stay focused on certain tasks. And there's things like diet and exercise, and maybe meditation, that can also help her holistically feel more centered and at ease."

"I've tried meditation," Zee said. "I fell asleep."

"Well, like anything else, meditation is a practice. It can take some time to get the hang of it."

The Carmichaels looked at one another. Mr. Carmichael reached out behind Zee for Mrs. Carmichael's shoulder and gave it a squeeze. "Is this going to impede her ability to succeed here at school?" he asked.

"It doesn't have to. A strong plan to help diagnose and manage her condition will be key. For one, confirming her diagnosis both here and with her doctor will help. Then if we can work together to help Zee be in tune with what's causing her anxiety and give her tools to help her manage these symptoms, I think she'll be fine. It's just a matter of knowing how to set her up for success," Dr. Banks said.

"All right," Mrs. Carmichael said. "So what now?"

"Let's continue with the journaling exercises and have Zee start honing in on a few exercises to help her anxiety. I'll keep you posted on her progress weekly and let you know if there's anything specific we should try next. But I warn you that a complete diagnosis and treatment plan may take some time to nail down as we do some tests and continue to assess Zee. Does that sound good for everyone?"

"Okay," Mrs. Carmichael said. "So long as long as we're not medicating our child. That is just something I don't want to consider."

"I completely understand," Dr. Banks said. "Zee, do you feel okay about things?"

"I guess," Zee said. "So will I see you next week alone?"

"Yes, Zee. We can meet at the same time next week. Sound good?"

"Okay," Zee said. She turned to her mother. "Mom, I'm sorry I didn't want to burden you with this."

Mrs. Carmichael gave Zee a big squeeze with one arm. "Darling, you can tell me anything, no matter what. You're not a burden, you're a blessing."

Zee squeezed her mother back, melting into her arms. For the first time in at least a week, Zee felt a sense of reassurance that things, including her mental health issues, her status with her teachers, and her relationship with her first boyfriend, might turn out better than she expected.

• • •

Zee texted Chloe as soon as her parents left campus.

Zee

> So I just left therapy with
> my parents. Good times.

Chloe

> Whoa, what happened?

Zee

> I guess my parents wanted to know what was wrong with me. Doc says I might have ADHD.

Chloe

> Really? Well, that's not surprising.

Zee nearly dropped the phone when she read her friend's response.

Zee

> Really?! Thanks, friend!

Chloe

> It's not a bad thing! I just meant you do get distracted easily.

Zee

> That doesn't mean I'm weird!

Chloe

> I didn't say you were!

Zee

> I don't want to have a disorder.

Chloe

> It's not a big deal. Some of the smartest and most creative people I know have ADHD.

Like who?

Like everyone in Hollywood!

Oh right. Everyone on the Internet too?

Pretty much!

I'm just kidding. Point is, many people have it, and it doesn't have to be a bad thing. How did your mom take it?

She was mad she didn't know about me seeing a therapist earlier.

I'm surprised your dad didn't tell her before. Good to know he can keep a secret though. Next time I need to not tell my parents something, he's my first call.

Like about how much money you really spent to get those box braids done for your soccer meet?

Chloe

Yeah. Dad still hasn't realized I split the amount on two credit cards.

Zee

I can't believe you HAVE two credit cards.

Chloe

One was in his name. Anyway, so what now?

Zee

Journal. Try to meditate. I dunno.

Chloe

Right. You'll be fine.

Zee sat up in her chair as she remembered something.

Zee

Oh, forgot to mention I saw Archie the other day. Had the talk. Didn't go well.

Chloe

> What happened?

Zee

> Suggested we tell each other at the same time how we feel. So we did. He wants to be together. I want to be just friends. Awkward.

Chloe

> Oof. Are you still speaking?

Zee

> Barely.

Chloe

> Well, it could work out better for your health. Now you'll have more time to journal and meditate.

Zee put her phone down and sighed. At least that was true.

8

HEADLINES AND HEADACHES

Zee still read *The Brookdale Beat*, the school newspaper at Brookdale Academy, because Chloe was the editor in chief. Zee loved reading Chloe's musings about celebrities, social media influencers, and the students at Brookdale Academy. She admired her best friend's talent for putting together a good story. Zee never really thought of herself as a journalist—more as a creative writer whose best work was in the form of poetry or songs. But someone else on campus saw potential in Zee's ability to tell a story.

Zee was in line for a smoothie one afternoon in the main dining hall, patiently waiting and thinking about a new song, when someone tapped her on the shoulder. Zee turned around.

"Are you Zee Carmichael?" said a girl with brown hair held back by a blue headband and fair skin. She was holding a few books in her arm as if she hadn't had time to find a seat yet.

"Yes, I am."

"I'm Ella Adams," the girl said. "I'm the editor for *The Hollows Post*."

"Oh, hi! Funny, I just browsed the website yesterday. How are you?" Zee said.

Ella grinned. "Great! We covered the talent show the other day and you did an amazing job. Did you see our story?"

"Yeah, you included my picture! My mom saved a copy of that issue and framed it," Zee said.

"That's so lovely," Ella said, smiling. "My mum still saves every issue I've done too. I told her she could save space and just look at the website instead."

Zee was next in line to order. "I'll have the green smoothie with cucumber, pineapple, and mint," she told the man behind the counter. She turned to Ella. "Did you want something?"

"Oh no, that's okay," Ella said politely. "Actually, I wanted to ask you something. I saw you were in Izzy Matthews's blog about the talent show. And obviously you're a great songwriter. But I wondered if you did any other type of writing. We're looking for new writers for the newspaper. Have you ever thought about writing for the newspaper?"

Zee was surprised at Ella's offer. "Um, no, I haven't."

"We're looking to expand our arts section and include different voices. Would you be interested in writing for us?" Ella asked.

Zee raised her eyebrows. "But what would I write? Songs? Poetry?"

"Sure! Or maybe you could interview some students you know already. You could, say, interview Izzy about her photography project. Like how she put it together and what work went into it. We want to include more stories of how our talented students do what they do."

Zee knew she could ask her friends questions about stuff

they liked to do. All she had to do was type out Izzy's answers. How hard could it be? "Okay, sounds like fun!"

"We meet twice a week after school," Ella said. "How about you drop by the writing lab tomorrow and we can talk more about it?"

"Okay," Zee said.

"Great! See you tomorrow," Ella said.

The young man working the smoothie machine handed Zee a frosty green drink. "See you then," Zee said to Ella, grabbing her smoothie and smiling as she sipped.

• • •

Zee arrived at the busy headquarters for *The Hollows Post*, a beautiful, well-lit conference room full of brand-new computers and printers. Oversized clippings from past issues of the paper and group photos of previous student staffers hung on the walls. In the corner, a sectional and long table allowed people to gather and review printed pages or brainstorm story ideas. Zee slowly walked around the room, looking for Ella.

"Zee!" Ella called out from behind one of the computers. She was looking over the shoulder of one of the paper's columnists. "Give me one second. Have a seat on the couch there."

Zee moved toward the sectional and took a seat. She picked up an issue of the paper that was laid out on the table. The cover included a story on the winning record of The Hollows tennis team with a picture of the team's smiling faces, and a story on the cafeteria's new fall menu featuring vegetables from the campus garden.

"Today's issue," Ella said as she sat down next to Zee with a notebook and pen. "I stayed up late getting in that story on the tennis team at the last minute. How are you? Thanks for coming by."

"Sure, no problem," Zee said. "How often do you publish issues?"

"We do one a week," Ella said. "And we update the website and social media daily."

Ella put down her notebook next to her on the couch. "Like I mentioned before, we're basically looking for people to do one-on-one interviews with other students on campus about their creative pursuits. We thought you could talk to kids with more unique creative talents and find out what they are working on, what they're into, their passions and stuff."

Zee nodded. "Sure, that sounds great."

"We also think that you could have an interesting perspective since you're a new student here on campus. How

long have you been here? You've just arrived this fall, right?"

"Yeah, I moved from California."

"Ah," Ella said. "California! Hollywood! Santa Monica! Malibu! Calabasas!"

"Um, yes," Zee said. "But not everyone is a Kardashian."

"Right," Ella said. "I saw that you were in Izzy Matthews's exhibition too."

Zee nodded. Izzy had taken her photo for a collection of student portraits for the Festival. "Yes, she's a talented photographer," Zee said.

"She is," Ella agreed. "Maybe we could use some of her photographs in the paper."

"That could be cool," Zee said. "I can interview her and see if she has any new photos to share."

Ella nodded. "So, do you have any siblings?"

"Yeah, I have an older brother who's in college, and I have twin siblings at home."

"Nice," Ella said, sounding more like a reporter. "What does your dad do?"

"He's in advertising. That's why we came to England, because he got a new job at a company here."

"Ah, right. Cool. And your mum?" Ella reached for her phone. "Hold on, your mum's that influencer, right? What's her handle again?"

Zee's eyebrows raised in surprise. "TwobyCarmichael. How did you know that?"

"I think I saw you tagged on her feed or something. Two, like the number but spelled out? By... Carmichael..." Ella slowly said as she typed the handle into the Instagram app on her phone. "Look at this! Wow, your mum's pretty! And look at these cute twins!"

"Thanks," Zee said slowly, starting to feel like she was being interviewed for an article, not hired to do the interviewing.

Ella turned back to her. "So how often do you practice your music?"

"I write every day. And then I jam with other friends when I can."

"Who are your mates?"

"Well, there's Jasper Chapman," Zee explained.

"Jasper. Year nine. Makes music. A gentleman, that Jasper."

"Yes. And—" Zee hesitated before naming Archie. He did help her a lot to frame her song for the Festival. And they had become good friends at one point. Maybe not at *this exact moment*, but at some point. "And Archie Saint John."

Ella's face froze. "Archie? *The* Archie Saint John? Year nine?"

"Yep," Zee said. "He's great on guitar. He helped me with my Festival song."

"Interesting," Ella said. "I had no idea you were such close friends with Archie. I had no idea he had any close friends."

"Yeah, we're friends. Well," Zee stammered as she shifted in her seat, "maybe friends and more. We were like boyfriend girlfriend, but we're not anymore."

Ella shook her head. "You were? When?"

Zee realized she had said too much. Why was she revealing everything to the editor of the school newspaper? "It's complicated. No need to get into it now."

"Right," Ella said, somewhat stunned by this bit of news. "Anyway, you could start profiling anybody who is interested. Maybe we should start with Izzy and we could reprint some of her photographs in the paper. Or maybe she has another photo project coming up that we could reveal first."

"That'd be cool," Zee said. "Oh, we could interview my roommate, Jameela Chopra, about ballet in an upcoming issue."

"Great idea. She is a beautiful dancer." Ella looked at her watch then stood up suddenly. "I better get back to work. But let me know if you have any issues."

"Okay, great," Zee said. She was excited about the opportunity to write for the *Post*. It was a great way to meet new people and become connected with The Hollows student body. But that Ella sure asked a lot of questions. *I guess she is a journalist*, Zee thought.

• • •

With no meetups with Archie taking up her daily schedule, Zee was free to dive into her piece for *The Hollows Post*. She texted her friends and family about the offer to write for the paper. Then she went into the Zee Files and posted a selfie she snapped in front of one of the oversized issues of the *Post* that was hanging on the office walls.

Girls, guess what? I'm following in your footsteps! I'm interviewing students on campus about their hobbies for our arts section. First, I want to talk to Izzy Matthews about her photo exhibit.

Chloe wrote back first. *Oh my gosh, that's so great for you! So excited to give you some pointers on reporting, haha!*

Looks like we're all writers right now, Ally chimed in. Then she posted a link to her latest article for the literary journal she was working on. *This was published last week.*

Congrats, Ally! Zee wrote back. The title of the essay was "An American in Paris."

Ally added, *I talked about some of our shopping trip in the essay. Since we were three Americans in Paris that day, if you include your mom.*

Zee smiled as she typed. *Oh wow, Ally, that's so sweet! I'll read this for inspiration.*

Then Zee texted Izzy to schedule an interview for the story in *The Hollows Post*. She knew they'd have study group together this week, but Zee was too excited to wait and wanted to make sure Izzy could find the time in her busy schedule to do an interview. Izzy responded quickly.

Izzy

OMG... yes, of course! You know Mr. Hysworth wants me to photograph more kids and make this like an evolving exhibit that includes new students every semester? Crazy, right?!

Zee

That's awesome! And a perfect news hook for your story. Ella will be excited.

> How about after we study tomorrow we hang late to do the interview? I'll bring a bunch of photos and stuff that I've taken and we can pick the ones you want to use.

> Awesome! Can't wait!

Finally, Zee gave her parents a call. Her mother picked up the phone on the first ring. She could hear her twin siblings chatting in toddler-speak in the background.

"That's wonderful, darling," Mrs. Carmichael said at hearing the news about the article. "But you don't think this will be too much work for you given your classwork and therapy already?"

"No, Mom. It's just one story," Zee said. "And I'm interviewing Izzy, who I already know! This should be a piece of cake. I'll see how it goes, but I don't think it will be too much."

"Right. Okay, darling, keep me posted."

Mr. Carmichael was equally pleased and cautious when Zee told him. "You sure you're going to have time to do this and balance your studies?" he said.

"Yes, Dad, of course," Zee said. "Mom asked the same thing. It's just one story to start. I'll contribute more when I have the time."

"Okay," Mr. Carmichael replied. "Be careful. Great to see you're finding your way on campus. Proud of you."

Zee hung up with a smile on her face, though she did feel a bit nervous. Her mind swam with ideas and questions of what to ask Izzy, and she reached for a notebook to start writing.

• • •

Zee walked across the quad toward her study group, her backpack a little heavier from all the extra notes for her science project and English lit readings. Her head swirled with thoughts about her article and when she could fit writing the story in between her homework, researching her part of the oceans project she was doing with Jasper, and practicing her music. Just then, she heard a voice call from the street. "Hey, Cali."

Zee turned around and saw Archie there. "Hi, wow, I... Hi."

He looked at her. "Been a minute, yeah? How are you?"

"Good, things are good. What are you up to now?"

"I'm on my way back to the dorm. Got some work to do. Now that I have all of this new free time."

Zee's stomach clenched. "Oh, Archie. I never said we had to stop hanging out completely."

"Well, that's how it felt, friend."

"Archie—"

"Look, I don't want to fight," Archie said. "But you said let's be friends. So, friend, I gave you your space."

"Well, thanks, friend," Zee said slowly. "But friends still text each other once in a while. Or call. Or send an e-mail. Or hit 'like' on a post, geez."

"Fair," Archie said.

"So..." Zee said.

"So," Archie replied. Both of them stood there not knowing what to say next. So they said nothing. Then they laughed.

"I still miss you," Zee said.

"Miss you too," Archie said, smiling back at her. "So what's been going on?"

"I'm going to start writing for the school paper, so that's fun," Zee told him.

"*The Hollows Post*? Riveting copy," Archie quipped.

"Har har. I'm writing articles about other kids on campus for the arts section. I'm profiling Izzy first, because, well, as Ella implied, she is our most famous student here."

"Ella?" Archie repeated.

"Ella Adams. The *Post* editor."

Archie rolled his eyes. "Right, Ella."

"Do you know her?"

"I know her a bit. Not a lot. Anyway, Zee, I'm happy for you. If you're happy, I'm happy."

"Right," Zee said. "You sure?"

"Yeah," Archie said, rolling his eyes up toward the sky. "I'm happy for you. I think it's great."

"Thanks!" Zee said. She looked at her phone and felt her neck strain as the weight of her backpack grew heavier. "I guess I'll get back at it."

"Good to see you, Cali," Archie said, smiling at her.

"You too," she said. "Don't be a stranger."

Zee smiled as she walked away, feeling better about things with Archie. She looked back over her shoulder at him and saw that he was still looking at her, one half of his mouth lifted in a grin. Zee stopped walking, gave him a smile and a wave, and continued her way, her heart fluttering the whole time.

After some algebra and science homework, Zee interviewed Izzy at their study group about her process of photographing students and about her expanding photo exhibit. Izzy spoke fast and excitedly, then showed Zee a few new photos she had taken of herself, Jasper, and her roommate, Poppy. The photos made them all look like they'd just stepped out of a toothpaste commercial.

"Really, Izzy, fashion brands should ask you to shoot their holiday campaigns," Zee said, looking over the photos.

"That's my dream, to shoot big-time commercials," Izzy said.

"Maybe my dad can be some help with that," Zee said.

"Ooh, there's an idea!" Izzy said.

After taking pages of notes and recording their conversation on her phone, Zee went back to her room and threw herself into the assignment, writing about Izzy's process, her vision for the school photo exhibit, and what it's like working with The Hollows students as subjects. Zee cranked out 500 words for the story without a break, then read and reread what she typed in an effort to have every word sound just perfect.

When Zee finally finished, it was past 11:30 p.m. Jameela was already asleep in her bed, the covers tightly tucked under her chin and an eye mask resting on her face to block out ambient light. Zee closed her laptop and crawled into bed. She fell asleep quickly, exhausted but feeling good about the story.

• • •

At 7:45 a.m., Zee shifted over in her bed, lazily opened one eye, and saw the steam of light pour into her room. It seemed awfully bright for it to be...

"Oh. My. LANTA!" she cried, throwing the blanket off and sitting up quickly. "I'm so late!"

Zee ran to the bathroom and splashed cold water on her face, then quickly threw her hair up into a loose bun, smudged some lip balm on her lips, grabbed her uniform blazer, and headed out for class. She ran into Jasper on the quad. "Hey, Zee, got those notes for our oceans project?" he asked.

Ugh, Zee thought. She totally forgot to do the research for her part of the project that he had asked for. She had been so consumed with her article on Izzy that she'd pushed aside the oceans assignment. "Oh no, Jas, I forgot! I'll have it tonight. I promise."

"Tonight?" Jas exclaimed. "We need to be prepared for class in an hour. Mr. Roth is going to ask if we've decided what we're doing for our fundraiser."

"We'll be okay, promise," Zee said, though she knew she had disappointed Jas, and without a plan for their oceans project she would soon disappoint Mr. Roth too. A jolt of worry went through her body as she digested the consequences of working late on her story for the school newspaper.

Maybe I shouldn't have signed up for the school paper with all I have going on, she thought as she rushed to class.

9

ALL TOGETHER NOW

"So you know what's coming up in a few weeks?" Tom began as he sat down at the group's regular table in the cafeteria. Jameela chewed her salad while Jasper slurped on his chicken noodle soup.

"A full moon?" Zee asked.

"Good guess, my friend," Tom said. "That's next week. I was referring to the annual Harvest Dance."

Zee looked at her friends. She didn't recall this event on her official school calendar. "Is that a thing?"

"It's a thing all right," Jameela said. "Everyone goes to the Harvest Dance. It's fall themed, and there's food and fun games. It raises money for charity too, usually a local one. I love a good dance." Jameela put down her fork. "Any excuse to dress up in a fancy dress is brilliant."

"Well, this will be my first one. I mean, everything this year is my first, really," Zee said. She looked at Jameela, uneasy about asking the next question. "So, um, do we take dates to this Harvest Dance?"

"That's usually the case, Zee," Jameela said. She looked at Tom, then looked away quickly before he could notice. "You'll have Archie, yes?"

Zee looked down at her plate, then looked away from the table. "Not necessarily."

"Why not?" Jameela said. "Is he out of town again?"

"Not exactly," Zee said. "We're not, like, together anymore. I don't think."

"I thought you were boyfriend and girlfriend," Jasper said, raising an eyebrow.

"Yes, that was true. But now we're more just friends. Or whatever. It's complicated."

"Complicated already?" Jameela said. "You two were dating for, like, a week!"

"Yeah, I know, it's just, you know," Zee said as she grew more uncomfortable talking about Archie. "Anyway, school dance! So what's it all about? Is there a band? Should I perform?"

"There is usually a DJ," Tom explained. "Like one of the guys from one of the upper levels usually spins. Jasper, you going to work the sound system on this one?"

Jasper looked away from Zee. "I might. Depends on the DJ."

"Right," Tom said. "And as for dates, I'm not sure." Tom looked briefly at Jameela, then looked away shyly. Both of them looked down at their meals.

"Maybe I won't go," Jasper said. Everyone looked at him. "Maybe I'll volunteer to do the sound so I can just stay backstage."

"That doesn't sound like much fun," Zee said.

"It's more fun than worrying about a date," Jasper said. "Who knows, maybe I can help bring in some special entertainment or something."

Just then, Archie walked by their table and overheard the group talking about the entertainment for the fall dance. "Maybe I'll actually do a little something on stage this year since I missed the Creative Arts Festival," he interjected. He slid into the seat next to Zee. "Hello, Cali."

"That's not the special entertainment I had in mind," Jasper said.

"Hello, Archie," Zee said.

"You planning to go to this Harvest affair?" Tom asked Archie.

"Indeed I am."

"Are you taking a date?" Tom asked.

"Guess that's yet to be determined," Archie said, looking directly at Zee.

The awkwardness could be cut with the biodegradable wood cutlery included with school meals. Zee chewed her food slowly, barely tasting her burrito. Jameela eyes bounced between Archie and Zee, but avoided Tom. Jasper slurped his soup as he avoided looking at Zee and Archie. Finally, Tom broke the silence.

"Okay," Tom said. "Maybe we should make this easy. Why don't we all just go together, but as friends? We can go as a group, and that way nobody will have to worry about who's taking who where."

Everybody let out a sigh of relief at the same time.

"That sounds lovely," Jameela said.

"We'll all meet up at the dance and hang out together. Since that's what we'd end up doing anyway," Tom continued. "So I'll have no date, but really four dates. That is, if you're in, Archie."

Zee felt a wave of calm come over her. She would have gone with Archie to the dance if he asked, but she also wanted to spend time with her friends. And she knew if she were Archie's date, he would have swept her to some private corner all night away from her friends. Particularly away from Jasper.

"That's the perfect plan," Zee said happily.

"It's all right," Archie said. "So we'll all have four dates. Does that mean I have to get you all flowers?"

"None for me, thank you," Jasper said. "I'm allergic."

"No, you're not," Zee said to him. "But I like flowers."

Archie looked at Zee. "Roses are red, violets are blue. I want to go to this dance, will you come with me too?"

"Awww," Zee said. "I'll go with you. And the gang."

Archie looked at Zee. "Deal." Then he looked at Tom and Jasper. "Sorry, mates, gonna save my pennies to get roses for my Cali."

"I'm crushed," Tom said.

"Me too," Jameela said.

Tom looked at Jameela and smiled. "Don't worry, you'll still get flowers." Jameela blushed.

"I have an idea!" Zee said excitedly. She turned to Jameela. "Why don't we go to London to look for dresses for the dance? We can stay the night at my place in Notting Hill. I'm sure my mom would love to have you. She's been asking about you for weeks. I can invite Izzy too."

"That's a fun idea," Jameela said.

"And that will even out the group too," Jasper said. "Three girls, three boys, all friends. Done."

"Right," Zee said. "And you can meet my twin siblings, Jameela. They are the cutest little munchkins. It'll be so much fun. We'll leave Friday night, go to London on Saturday, shop all day, and then go back to Notting Hill to spend the night. And then come back early Sunday." Then a thought hit her. "Oh, will you miss ballet practice?"

Jameela said excitedly, "Works for me, but let me check." She fished out a notebook from her backpack to check her schedule. "Well, look at that, I actually have a free weekend. Ms. Duckett is going out of town on family matters. I'm in."

• • •

After dinner, everyone returned to their respective dorms. Archie walked out with the group and for the first time in a long while did not walk Zee back to the dorm, instead leaving her with Jameela. As Zee walked across the quad with her roommate, she turned back once to Archie, just to get one last glance of him. He didn't turn back around to her. She walked on with Jameela, slightly disappointed.

Back at the dorm room, Zee got into her pajamas and sat in her bed reading over her art history notes. Right before she was about to turn off her nightlight and end her study session, her phone buzzed. A text message from Archie was waiting.

Archie

> How's working on the school paper going?

Zee

> Turned in my first story. Now working on homework. You?

Archie

All good. I don't want to interrupt.

Zee kept texting. Tonight, she didn't mind the interruption.

Zee

It's okay. What are you up to?

Archie

Guitar playing. Thinking of you. Friend.

Zee

Yes, we are friends. For now.

Archie

Friends who go to dances together.

Friends who go to dances together with other friends.

Right.

He sent a short audio clip. Zee clicked play, and Archie's voice sang in her ear:

"Roses are red, violets are blue.
You stole my heart and broke it in two.
Picked up the pieces and glued them tight.
Won't let go of her without a fight."

Zee didn't know whether to cry or be flattered. She really liked Archie. She missed him. And her unique bond with one of the most good-looking but most elusive guys on campus made her feel pretty special. Zee smiled and listened to the audio clip three times. She responded the only way she thought could be fitting, with five heart emojis.

Night, Cali, Archie texted.

10

CAMPING IN NOTTING HILL

Sitting at her desk in her dorm room, Zee had her nose deep into her science project. She somehow convinced Mr. Roth to give her and Jasper an extra day to come up with a fundraising idea to help clean up the oceans. Zee thought about having a coffeehouse cleanup where she could perform a live concert either on a beach or in conjunction with a beach organization, and then have the proceeds from tickets go toward a beach-cleanup effort. While she was in the middle of writing, a notification popped up from Ally on her phone.

Ally

> I'm at a loss on what I should write about this week for the literary journal.

Zee

> Really? I thought that your life as an American in Paris is what they were looking for.

Ally

Yeah, but I haven't really done anything exciting in weeks. I literally go to school and come home. I haven't even been to my favorite coffee shop in a while.

Zee

You can't let the streets of Paris go too long without the Ally charm.

Ally

My dad's been working like mad, so we haven't had much time to hit the streets.

An idea struck Zee right then. She got excited as she typed.

Zee

That sounds like a good excuse to come see me in London this weekend. I'm having a few friends over to shop for dresses for this Harvest Dance thing we have coming up. The whole school goes. Anyway, why don't you come so you can meet everybody?

Ally

I don't want to impose. It sounds like cool bonding time with your school friends.

No, silly! It'll be nice to have you, and nice to have my old pal with me in London. You can come hang out with everyone at my place. We'll do some shopping and you'll spend the night.

There was a short pause before Ally responded.

Ally

Sounds like fun. Let me ask my dad.

Zee

We can pick you up from the train station, and my parents will be here the entire time, so no worries.

Ally

Okay. I'll let you know if my dad says yes.

Zee

Awesome! See? Then you'll have something to write about for your literary journal. The American in Paris gets out of town to reunite with her friend the American in London!

• • •

Jameela usually stayed late on Fridays to practice ballet, and if she went home, she left on Saturday morning. But with her ballet instructor out of town, Jameela's weekend was free, so for the first time on a Friday, Zee and Jameela left the dorm for a weekend at the same time.

"I may have to do some stretching in your living room at some point, so don't be alarmed," Jameela told Zee.

"We have plenty of space," Zee said.

With their bags in hand, the girls headed to the front gate and checked out with the headmaster. Izzy met them there, her monogrammed weekend bag slung over her shoulder.

"Thanks for the invitation, Zee! Girls' road trip! So excited!" Izzy said.

"Well, now that I've been to your home, I get to show you mine," Zee said.

As they chatted, a black sedan pulled up to curb and Mrs. Carmichael, well dressed in a pair of wide-legged pants and a camel cape, stepped out from the back door. "Darlings!" she exclaimed, and excitedly waved the girls over.

"Hi, Mom," Zee said, walking toward her mother, who kept her arms out wide enough to give all the girls a hug at the same time. The girls returned the gesture.

"I had so many fun things planned for us," Mrs. Carmichael said. "And Camilla will watch the twins all day tomorrow so we can shop as long as we need!"

The driver helped Mrs. Carmichael and the girls load their bags into the trunk. Then they all climbed into the backseats of the sedan. As they drove away from the front gate, Mrs. Carmichael pulled out her phone and held it up to grab a selfie with all the girls together.

"Mom, we just got in the car!" Zee said.

"I know, and this is the kickoff to a fabulous weekend, so I want to capture it!"

"Looks like we've got two famous influencers on board," Jameela giggled.

"If you tag me in the photo, Mrs. Carmichael," Izzy said, "I can repost it on my feed too!"

"Perfect!" Mrs. Carmichael said. She clicked on her phone and looked up. "So, tell me all about this dance."

The girls excitedly filled in Mrs. Carmichael on the Harvest Dance details, including the fall-themed snacks and the activities.

"Sounds amazing," Mrs. Carmichael said. "And are you girls planning to take dates to this dance?"

"Mo-ooommm!" Zee said. "We all decided not to take dates. Tom, Jasper, Archie, and the three of us are going as one big group."

"I see," Mrs. Carmichael said. "How modern of you."

"Well, considering that Zee broke up with—" Jameela began.

"Considering that we just didn't want to deal with dates," Zee hurriedly cut Jameela off, giving her a look.

"Right," Jameela said, playing along.

"Dates are a hassle," Izzy said. "Besides, I'll be too busy filming for my vlog to deal with a date."

"Speaking of filming, Izzy, will you be filming the sleepover for your YouTube channel?" Mrs. Carmichael asked.

"Some things, sure."

"Well, just know you can film whatever you want at our house to put on your channel. I'm open to it!"

"Thanks, Mrs. Carmichael," Izzy said. "I brought my big

camera, so I could even shoot some portraits."

"Oh, that would be lovely! Maybe I should put on some makeup and model for you. You are quite the photographer."

"Mom, really?" Zee said, embarrassed. "Maybe Izzy wants to take a break. And don't force her to take your picture, that's weird."

"It's okay. I'd be honored to take your photo, Mrs. Carmichael," Izzy said.

"How sweet. Now, what kind of dresses are you all thinking about for the dance? Zee, I might have something in my closet you might like."

"Really?" Zee perked up. "I do love vintage."

"I'd like something super boho," Izzy said. "And lace."

"Oh, that sounds pretty," Mrs. Carmichael said.

"I'd like something classic," Jameela said. "Something tailored, something black. You can't go wrong with a little black dress."

"Nope," Mrs. Carmichael said. "You're never too young for a little black dress either. Even Phoebe, Zee's little sister, has one."

The sedan pulled up to the Carmichaels' Notting Hill home, and the girls eagerly hopped out. The driver helped them with their bags to the door and Mrs. Carmichael led the girls in. "We're here!" Mrs. Carmichael announced loudly.

The twins and their nanny, Camilla, were in the kitchen, so Mrs. Carmichael hurried to see them. Jameela and Izzy looked around the front room where the family photos hung on the walls and sat on the front desk. "This is really nice, Zee," said Izzy.

"Thanks," Zee said. Looking around, she noticed a few new

additions in the house, like a new vase set up in the window and a new side table near the couch. A plush pink knit blanket was also tossed over the back of one of the couches.

"Girls, come this way. I have a few surprises for you!" Mrs. Carmichael called out. The girls made their way into the kitchen, where Zee's baby twin siblings, Phoebe and Connor, scooted around with small toy cars while Camilla prepared dinner. Zee gave Camilla a nervous wave as she walked in. Then she turned to her mom who stood with four small bags on the counter. Each one had one of the girls' names on it.

"I got you ladies a few small things for your sleepover tonight. I just got so excited when Zee told me you all were going to come for the weekend," Mrs. Carmichael said with a smile.

Inside each shopping bag were striped flannel pajamas, a pair of fluffy slippers, and a sparkly makeup bag containing an eye mask and a small nail polish.

"Aww, Mrs. Carmichael, thank you!" Izzy cried.

Zee was stunned. "Yeah, Mom, thanks for the gifts," Zee said slowly.

Jameela and Izzy tried on their slippers. "They fit perfectly!" Izzy said.

Jameela's eyes grew wide as she unfolded the pajamas. "Oh my, these are great. And so my style. I want to try these on right now. Where's your bathroom?"

"First door on the right," Mrs. Carmichael said, pointing down the hallway.

Izzy artfully laid out the goods from the gift bag onto the floor and took a photo with her phone. "Gotta 'gram this!"

Mrs. Carmichael looked happy. "Tag me in the photo, dear,

so I can see and repost obviously! Oh, the Mummy Mums will love this."

"Who are the Mummy Mums?" Izzy asked.

"Her fancy mom friends," Zee answered. She raised an eyebrow as she looked at her mother. The gift bags were a lovely touch, but she wondered if she only did it so Izzy would post about them. Or to show them off to her mom friends.

Jameela came back out of the bathroom. "They fit perfectly," she said. "And they're so soft! These might be my new favorites."

"Fantastic!" Mrs. Carmichael said. "I think they'll go lovely with... this!" She pulled back the shades that covered the sliding patio door outside, revealing the surprise: their garden decorated for the ultimate glamping sleepover.

Set up outside was a large tent covering the main area of the garden, roomy enough for the girls to sleep inside. There were four individual large air mattresses covered with fluffy blankets and pillows in pastel shades. Beside the tent, the outdoor dining table was dressed with oversized coffee mugs and a serving platter full of pumpkin-spiced cookies, chocolates, graham crackers and marshmallows for s'mores, and apples and caramel dip. Fairy lights were hung on the tent and around the door frame, giving the area a warm glow. The girls walked out to a portable firepit, their eyes glowing from the flame.

"I know it's getting quite chilly on these crisp fall evenings in London, so I had this outdoor campfire thing set up here," Mrs. Carmichael said. "We could roast marshmallows, and you girls can hang out here in the evening and talk and gossip and gab. And it's not too cold out tonight, though I can bring you extra blankets."

Izzy looked around the garden with wide eyes. "This looks amazing! I want to move in here!"

Zee could not believe her eyes. She liked glamping. But she also missed her own bed, which was just upstairs. *Do I have to sleep out here too?* she wondered.

"All right, ladies, we have dinner planned in a bit. I hope you're hungry. Zee, why don't you show them around?" Mrs. Carmichael suggested.

Zee walked in front of her friends and made her way toward the stairway leading to the upstairs bedrooms.

"So does your mum know about Archie?" Izzy asked once the three of them were alone.

"No," Zee said.

"Really? You never told her?"

"To be honest, no. We got together and then broke up so fast that I barely had time to have a relationship to talk about."

"Well, that's true. But still, keeping secrets from your mother is never good."

"It's not a secret," Zee said. "It's just news that wasn't worth sharing. Anyway, now Archie and I are just friends. More important are things like my work on the paper and stuff... Oh! I finished that profile of you, Izzy. Ella said it was great."

"Ooh, thanks, I can't wait to read it!" Izzy said.

"C'mon, let me show you upstairs," Zee said, taking the girls up to the second floor, where her parents', the twins', and Camilla's bedrooms were, then kept going toward the stairs to the third floor where her bedroom was.

She opened the door. "This is it. My room," Zee said.

The room was tidy, Zee's bed tightly made with smooth bedding. A blue bean bag chair sat underneath the window, perfectly fluffed. Her denim jacket had been carefully draped over her desk chair, and her picture frames sparkled on top of the desk. It was as if Camilla had been in to tidy. That thought shook Zee. *Does she go through my stuff when I'm not here?*

"Cool," Izzy said as she and Jameela walked in and looked around. "California shabby chic! Is this your memorabilia from your band in California?"

"Yeah, that's us in California," Zee said, looking over Izzy's shoulder at a photo frame she held. Zee had played with Chloe and Ally in a band called The Beans back in California. Zee thought wistfully about her good friends and the fun they had as she looked at the photo.

"That's awesome!" Izzy picked up a framed photo of The Beans taken at the television studios of KTLA-TV, right before Zee left for England. "Is this from a TV show?"

Zee smiled. "Oh yeah, we were on a show called *Good Morning L.A.* there."

Jameela looked around the room. "It's all quite... it's quite you."

"Thanks, Jameela. I'm not sure what that means, but okay. Anyway," Zee said. "It looks like we can all spend the night either here or in the faux campfire tent situation my mom set up on the freezing cold patio. Whichever you like."

"I actually wouldn't mind a little campout," Izzy said as she looked at more photos on Zee's desk. "Besides, like she said, it's not that cold out, and with the firepit I bet we'll be cozy."

"Sleeping out under the stars in Notting Hill," Jameela said with a sigh. "A first for everything."

"If you really want to," Zee said with a shrug. "My mom would be thrilled. Don't be surprised if she hovers over us in the middle of the night to take photos of us sleeping for her feed."

The girls went back downstairs where Camilla was helping Mrs. Carmichael assemble dinner. As they bustled around the kitchen, Mr. Carmichael came in. "Wow, a house full of the most talented students I know," he said. "Ladies."

"Hi, Dad," Zee said, giving him a hug. "Did you help Mom put together all of this camping stuff outside?" Zee asked.

Mr. Carmichael looked out to the patio. "Your mother had me stringing fairy lights until 10 p.m. We're lucky it didn't rain."

While the girls hovered around the kitchen, Zee walked

toward the front room with her cell phone. She had one notification—from Chloe. *How's the best party in town this weekend?* the text read.

Zee had promised to video call Chloe from the gathering so that she could feel like she was there with the gang. But for some reason, Zee didn't feel like part of the gang either.

Zee texted back: *It's madness. My mother has really done it.* She checked and saw it was 8 p.m., which would mean it was morning in Los Angeles where Chloe was.

Two minutes later, Chloe called Zee. "What happened?"

Zee's feelings rose up into her throat as she heard her friend's voice. "My mother, obsessed with all things social media, has totally co-opted the sleepover to make it all about her," Zee said in a rush.

"What do you mean?"

"She had gift bags with pajamas and eye masks and slippers waiting for us, and she designed a Pinterest board–type backyard sleepover thing with tents and a firepit and stuff. It's supposed to be a casual sleepover with a few friends, and she has turned it into a production. Like, I just want to sleep in my own bed."

"It doesn't sound half-bad to me. I mean, I wish I were there with you. Send me some pictures!" Chloe said.

"I know. I miss you," Zee said. "But where's my old mom? My old mom would never throw some over-the-top, keep-up-with-the-Joneses–type sleepover. She wasn't on Instagram. She wasn't doing all this stuff to impress other people."

Just then, Mrs. Carmichael walked in the room behind Zee to see if her daughter was okay. She overheard Zee on the phone with someone and stopped.

"That can't be true," Chloe said.

Zee clutched the phone to her ear. "It's true. If she takes one more picture with Izzy, I think I will throw her phone into the Thames River."

"I wish I were there. Send me more pictures."

"Chloe, whose side are you on?"

"I'm not on any side! Look, try to relax. I think that your mom is just being nice and trying to help you impress your friends. Let her be your mom. Let her have some fun with it."

Zee sighed. "I know, but this is just—it seems very over the top. In California, Mom was super chill. But since we got here, everything seems a little more, you know, ridiculous."

"I think you need to just kind of let your mom be a mom. She's excited for you, she's an influencer now, so everything is content. This is good for you. You've got the cool mom now. Everyone wants to have the cool mom," Chloe said.

"I guess."

"And this sleepover sounds super amazing. I totally wish I were there."

"Thanks. Miss you."

As Zee hung up, she turned back toward the hallway to rejoin the crew in the kitchen. She almost ran face first into her mom standing at the doorway with a disappointed look on her face. *Oh, no. Did she hear me complaining?* Zee wondered.

"Is there a problem, Zee?"

Zee stood stunned. *Yep, she heard me. Ugh.* "Mom. I just..."

"Your friends are waiting for you on the patio."

Zee looked at her mother's face. Her eyes were fixed forward, her mouth tense. Mrs. Carmichael looked like she was holding back tears, but because she wanted everything to look perfect for the evening, she held in her disappointment and sadness for later.

Zee walked slowly by her mother. "I'm sor—"

"Your friends are waiting," Mrs. Carmichael said again.

Zee walked ahead of her mother into the kitchen area, feeling guilty for having spoken badly about her mother and then being caught doing so. Mrs. Carmichael walked up the stairs toward the bedrooms, not turning back to Zee.

11

SHOP TILL YA DROP

The girls roasted marshmallows and gossiped until nearly midnight about school, music, and the future of a few popular Hollows students. They chatted until they finally got too tired and fell asleep under the fluffy blankets.

Zee woke to a text from Ally, whose dad had agreed to let her visit Zee in London: *Leaving Paris now. See you in a few hours.* As the sun warmed the morning fall London air, Zee, Jameela, and Izzy crawled out from the oversized tent and shuffled quickly back into the house with blankets draped around their shoulders. Camilla was preparing a buffet-style breakfast of cereals, eggs, breads and jams, and fruits.

"Did you sleep well?" Mrs. Carmichael asked as she entered the kitchen.

"Yes!" Izzy and Jameela enthusiastically replied.

"I have a crick in my neck," Zee said.

"Sorry to hear that, darling," her mother said.

"You know I don't sleep well in strange beds."

"What strange bed? I put your blankets and pillow

from your bed upstairs down on the inflatable bed," Mrs. Carmichael said.

"But the mattress wasn't the same. It just felt different."

"Maybe breakfast will help," Mrs. Carmichael responded. She turned to Izzy and Jameela. "Camilla has cooked up a feast this morning. I'll be back shortly. Ally's train just arrived."

As the twins sparred over a toy car on the living room floor, the girls munched on porridge and fresh fruit, eggs, and fresh juice. They had just uploaded photos of their breakfasts to their social media feeds (and the Zee Files, in Zee's case) when the front door locks jingled.

The girls all rushed to the door, Zee at the front, bounding through the long hallway to greet her BFF.

"Allyyyyy—" Zee said as the front door opened, then stopped dead in her tracks. A girl with a perfect blowout and a berry stain on her lips was standing before them in a striped boatneck top and wide-legged jeans. She looked perfectly pulled together, even for a casual Saturday.

"Made it! So good to see you," Ally said, hugging Zee.

"You did!" Zee said. "And you look so... grown up! Even more than last time."

"Must be the blowout," Ally said. "I just got a haircut."

No, it's something more, Zee thought, *but I just can't put my finger on it.*

"Ally's here!" Izzy called out from behind Zee, her phone camera held up to record Ally's welcome. "The gang's all here now! Welcome to London!"

"This is Izzy and Jameela," Zee introduced her old friend to her new friends, who at first glance were just as impressed with Ally's appearance as Zee was.

"Hi! So nice to meet you," Ally said. "Zee talks about you both a ton."

"And same about you," Jameela said. "How was your ride in from Paris?"

"Fine," Ally said. "I had my headphones on the whole time."

"Always makes mass transit better," Jameela said.

"You must be hungry," Zee said. "Come in, let's get you a snack."

Zee watched Jameela and Ally as they walked shoulder to shoulder toward the kitchen. Izzy followed closely behind, recording for her vlog with her cell phone. Once in the kitchen, Mrs. Carmichael had a gift bag ready for Ally filled with the same pajamas, slippers, and beauty care the other girls received the night before. "Wow, best sleepover ever!" Ally said.

"So tell us all about life in Paris," Jameela said. "I love Paris. I did a dance camp there a few years back."

"It's all right. Lots of people, lots of cafés. Lots of people in cafés. And really great croissants."

"Right! I remember," Jameela said, intently listening to Ally's every word. Zee quietly watched them chat as Izzy recorded everything.

Mrs. Carmichael reappeared then with her purse. "Girls, ready for some shopping? Get your walking shoes on and your wallets ready!"

• • •

Walking the streets of Notting Hill, the girls and Mrs. Carmichael took in the lights and sounds of the neighborhood while debating what dresses they should buy for the dance. Ally and Jameela hit it off well—surprisingly well, Zee thought—chatting and chuckling as they wandered down the shopping square. Their first stop was a boutique in the north of Notting Hill called Made, where Izzy had shopped before (and documented on her IG feed, including the prices, sizes, and reviews of all the items she bought). Izzy wanted something boho chic for the dance,and the store's lacy frocks fit the bill. She dashed around the clothing racks and quickly scooped up a handful of dresses, tried on each one, modeled them for Zee, Jameela, Ally, and Mrs. Carmichael, and filmed their reactions. Mrs. Carmichael gave chirpy commentary to each selection. "Oh, that looks lovely!" she said when Izzy tried on a purple maxi dress.

Finally, Izzy decided on a pink-blush number that made her eyes look bluer than usual. "I'll take this one!" Izzy declared.

At the next shop, Jameela found a classic black dress with puffed sleeves that fit her perfectly. "I know what I like," Jameela said. "I can spot it on a rack immediately."

"That looks amazing on you," Ally swooned.

"Thanks," Jameela swooned right back.

What is up with Jameela? Zee thought to herself. *She's never nice to strangers.*

In between finding their dresses, the girls looked for earrings and accessories, shoes, and other fun bits and bobs. Mrs. Carmichael dragged them into the Goop store to look at some of their beauty products ("This stuff is expensive!" Zee said as she looked at a bottle of skin cream. "At least it's nontoxic.") and Izzy found fun nail art sets while scoping out nail polish at a Boots outpost.

"Maybe I'll do some fun designs on my nails to match my dress," Izzy pondered.

But Zee hadn't yet found a dress to her liking. That is, not until they walked past a vintage boutique next to the stationers where Zee spotted the ultimate find in the window: a tea-length, pale lavender dress. It had cap sleeves with a soft neckline, and a tulle skirt. "Per-FECT!" Zee said.

She ran inside the store, disappearing before she could say "Excuse me" to her mother and friends.

"Helloooo!" she greeted the clerk behind the counter. "That dress is calling me!"

Zee snapped a few selfies of herself in the dress, one of which she sent to Chloe. Then she took the dress to the cashier, thanked her mother for paying for it ("It was eighty percent off the original retail price! Practically free!" Zee said.) and walked out with the perfect Harvest Dance dress in hand.

"That dress really is you, Zee," Jameela said. "Quite unique. I'm sure Archie will love it."

Zee laughed. "Thanks. I bought it for me," she said, "but if he likes it, he likes it."

• • •

After a full day of shopping, snacking, and walking past the colorful houses of Notting Hill, the girls and Mrs. Carmichael made it back home with arms full of dresses and accessories. Ally, Jameela, and Zee collapsed on the couches in the den to catch their breath. Suddenly Izzy spoke up: "Let's model our dresses for Ally! We can do a little catwalk down the hallway."

"Brilliant idea!" said Jameela.

"We need music!" Izzy said. "Zee, do you have anything fashion-show appropriate in one of your playlists?"

"Sure," Zee said, pulling up her music to find an up-tempo dance song. Izzy propped her phone on the counter so it could record the girls parading down the makeshift catwalk. Zee hit play on the music app, then the girls went to the far end of the hallway to the kitchen, tucked into private corners, slid on their dresses, and lined up out of Ally's sight.

"Ready, Ally?" Jameela called.

"Yes!" Ally said. "Start the show."

Zee sauntered out first. She walked down the hallway

with her hips swaying exaggeratedly left and right, bounding her head to the music. She pumped one fist in the air when she came to the entrance of the kitchen. "Wow! Zee, that's a great look!" Ally said. Zee smiled as she turned and walked off to the side of the kitchen.

Next, Jameela walked down the aisle, poised like a graceful swan prancing across an icy pond. Her lips were locked into a serious pout, making her jawline even more pronounced. She paused at the entrance and gave a duckface expression to one side, then the other. Ally took in the look from head to toe. "Chic!" Ally said. Then Jameela broke from her model character and smiled, tossed her long black hair over her shoulder, and pranced over toward Zee.

Finally, Izzy came dancing down the hallway in her pink floor-length lace boho gown, her long, blonde hair bouncing with every step and her blue eyes wide and focused down the hallway.

"Yes! Ally said. "That's perfect for you."

Izzy gave a peace sign as she stood in front of Ally, then floated to the side of the kitchen and picked up her phone. "Annnd I got that all on video, naturally!"

. . .

Later that evening, the girls huddled around the firepit outside on the patio dressed in their new pajamas and slippers, and snuggled under the oversized blankets. Jameela and Ally continued their conversation about dance, Paris, traveling, boys, and fashion that seemed to have begun since Ally first walked through the door. Ally even confided in Jameela about her parents' divorce during dinner. "It's been rough," Ally had told her, with Jameela nodding slowly.

As the girls roasted s'mores, Izzy asked Zee, "So what did happen between you and Archie?"

Just then, Mrs. Carmichael walked outside to refill the snacks. She leaned over the table by the firepit. "Girls, I have more popcorn on the way. And who's Archie, Zee? I've heard the name a few times but can't recall meeting him."

Zee stuffed a marshmallow into her mouth, trying to avoid answering the question. "Um, a friend," Zee said. The girls looked at one another.

"Sounds like he was more than a friend. Was he also a distraction from your schoolwork?"

"No, Mom. He helped me with my song for the Festival. We hung out a few times. But not much since."

Mrs. Carmichael raised an eyebrow. "I see. Will he be at this Harvest Dance?"

"Yes, Mom. But we're going as a group, not with dates."

"Right. Gotcha," she said, and made her way to the door. "We'll talk more about this later."

Zee melted into the soft inflatable bed she was sitting on. "Ugh," she groaned. "It's like no one wants me to be with Archie."

"She's your mum," Izzy said. "Of course she's going to be protective."

"Yeah, but none of my friends were supportive either."

"I was supportive," Izzy said.

"At first you were unimpressed."

"I was surprised. That's different."

"I thought it was too fast," Jameela said. "I've had pointe

shoes last longer than your relationship."

"Thanks, Jameela," Zee said sarcastically. "Archie is not a chill dude. He wanted all or nothing. And I didn't want to give him all."

"Right," Izzy said. "I get it."

"What did your therapist say about Archie?" Jameela blurted out.

Zee shook her head, confused. The only people in the house who knew about the therapist were her mother and Ally.

"You're seeing a therapist?" Izzy asked. "Are you all right?"

"Yes, I'm fine," Zee said, turning to Jameela. "How do you know I'm seeing a therapist?"

"I saw a notification on your computer a few weeks ago from Chloe asking how therapy was going," Jameela said. "I didn't say anything at the time because I didn't want you to think I was snooping."

Zee frowned. "Well, you kinda were."

"No, I accidentally saw a notification. And then I kept it to myself."

Zee started to feel queasy in the stomach. The more people who knew she was in therapy, the more people could judge her. And now not only did her perfect roommate know she needed a therapist, but YouTube's most perfect boarding school student, Izzy, also knew. "Great, now everyone knows I've got problems."

"Zee, you don't have problems, you have a therapist. There's nothing wrong with that," Izzy said.

"Yeah," Ally said. "I have parents who are splitting up. I don't know if I would say that's a problem since I want them to be happy, but it's not easy for me either."

"But having everyone know I'm seeing a therapist for my anxiety makes me more anxious," Zee said, her eyes downcast.

"Why are you so anxious?" Izzy asked.

Zee looked at her. "I don't know. I'm in a new city, in a new school, in a new bed, and that's an adjustment. Sometimes I don't sleep well because I feel like everything is just so unfamiliar and different. I don't even have my guitar here with me."

"I was wondering if you were still playing," Ally asked.

"It got lost in the move. I'm supposed to have it soon," Zee said. "Anyway, my schoolwork is harder than I planned. I'm not exactly getting stellar grades. I was anxious about the Festival, but that went all right, thank goodness. Then I finally became close friends with someone who appreciates my differences, and no one approves. It's just been a lot."

Jameela looked at Zee. "I understand. But you might be better off than you think. You are now one of the most popular kids at school after your Festival performance. And for having Archie Saint John as your boyfriend. Believe me, you fit in."

"You're also awesome!" said Ally.

"And talented!" said Jameela.

"And beautiful!" said Izzy.

Zee looked at her friends. "That's sweet," she said with a small grin. "Who needs therapy when I have you?"

"Besides," Izzy said. "I heard Archie was in therapy. I bet half the kids at school are in therapy. It might as well be an after-school sport."

"A few of the girls in ballet could use therapy," Jameela said. "Dealing with Ms. Duckett can drive you mad sometimes."

"Well, either way, I don't want the whole school to know, so if you can keep it to yourselves I'd be grateful," Zee said.

"Sure," Izzy said. "Pass me some graham crackers. S'mores make everyone feel better."

"Just don't get crumbs in your bed. That's the worst," Jameela said.

The girls snuggled under their blankets while they sipped hot chocolate and roasted marshmallows over the fire. Laughter filled the garden until near midnight, when they finally put out the flame on their portable firepit, zipped the tent closed, and fell asleep.

. . .

On Sunday the girls packed up their bags to get ready to head back to school. Zee's dad was going to take them back while Mrs. Carmichael decided to stay at home with the twins. She didn't want to cause any more friction with Zee that was already there and hung out in the kitchen while the girls piled their bags by the front door.

Zee went in the kitchen and found her mother feeding Phoebe while Connor played with his food. Zee walked over as Mrs. Carmichael spooned smashed peas into the toddler's mouth. "I think I was that age the last time I ate peas," Zee said.

"I think so too," Mrs. Carmichael said, not looking up at her daughter.

Zee took a seat at the table slowly as she eased into what she knew would be a hard conversation. "You know, this was a great sleepover, Mom. Thanks for doing all this stuff. I didn't know you had the time for such a production."

"You sure?" Mrs. Carmichael asked. "Or maybe it was too

much for you."

"Mom, I'm sorry. I didn't mean what I said on the phone to Chloe."

"What did you mean then?"

"I just felt a bit, I don't know, out of place in my own house," Zee said. "Here, I just wanted my own bed and my old blanket and my old pajamas, and to eat pizza and chill. I was looking forward to those comforts of home."

Mrs. Carmichael looked at Zee. She thought back to what Dr. Banks had said during their last meeting, how Zee's feelings of being out of place at school could carry over to her feelings at home.

"I'm sorry, I guess I didn't take that into consideration. I just wanted to impress your friends and set up a fun time for you all," Mrs. Carmichael said.

"I get it, Mom," Zee said.

"Did you have fun?"

"Yeah."

"Did your friends have fun?"

"Yes. I think they want to move into our backyard."

"We can keep the tent up," her mom said. "Might get cold out there in the dead of winter though."

Zee smiled at her. She hadn't meant to hurt her mom's feelings. "I did have a great time. I just, well... I should get a bit out of my comfort zone."

"Listen, I know things for you are challenging. At boarding school you're far away from home, both from California and from us. You're trying to figure out classes and make friends, and it's not all rosy all the time. And now you've got some therapist telling you that you might have ADHD. This is not easy stuff."

"I know."

"And I know you think I'm busy, but I will always have time for you. And you know you can tell me anything," Mrs. Carmichael said. "No matter what, I will always make time for you."

"Okay," Zee said. "So are we good?"

"Yes, darling. We're good."

• • •

With all the girls and their bags packed in the SUV, the first stop was the train station to drop off Ally. Mr. Carmichael parked in front of the station's main entrance. Zee opened the door to help Ally get out of the car. Jameela got out of the car right after. Ally grabbed her bag from the trunk and gave Jameela a heartfelt hug goodbye. Zee watched in surprise at how Jameela was instantly so friendly with Ally. "It was great meeting you!" Ally said.

"Yeah, you as well," Jameela said. "We have to keep in touch. I want to hear all about Paris."

The girls walked toward Zee, who stood there feeling like a third wheel.

"Thanks for inviting me, Zee. That was definitely the best sleepover I think we've ever had," Ally said.

"Yeah, it was something, right?"

"I should really come and visit you more often. Maybe I can come and visit you in the Cotswolds one weekend."

"That would be lovely! Maybe I can host the next sleepover," Jameela offered.

Zee couldn't believe what she was hearing. Jameela rarely talked about her home life and had never asked Zee to come and visit. But Jameela instantly connected with Zee's best friend. And Ally seemed to feel the same about Jameela.

"Bye for now, girls," Ally said as she walked toward the train station doors.

"Bye, Ally," Zee said. "I'll post pics in the File."

Jameela looked at Zee. "Maybe you should invite me into the Zee Files. I'd like to see the pictures and stuff you guys share. And I have some fun ones from the weekend."

Zee wrinkled her face. "First you know about therapy, and now the Zee Files? That's supposed to be a private thing between Ally, Chloe, and me."

"I know, but Ally told me you guys just mostly post photos."

"And personal writings, texts, and songs," Zee said. "Anyway, it's just for the three of us."

Zee turned to climb into the front seat of the SUV next to her dad, annoyed that Jameela was trying to infiltrate the one private space that she shared with her two closest friends from home. The Hollows schoolmates rode back to school tethered to their phones, sending Izzy all the photos they'd taken from the weekend. While Jameela and Izzy eagerly swooned at the happy memories they'd made at Zee's sleepover, Zee felt melancholy as she casually swiped through the photos of her and the girls at her house. *It was a great sleepover*, Zee thought distantly to herself.

Apparently Izzy agreed with Zee. "These photos," Izzy declared, "will make an amazing slideshow on my vlog!"

12

CHOOSING NEW FRIENDS

*A*fter Mr. Carmichael dropped the girls off on campus, Zee went somewhere private and sent Chloe a text: *I think Ally likes my roommate more than me.*

What in the world are you talking about? Chloe wrote back.

Zee called her friend in L.A. to respond, and Chloe picked up the phone on the first ring. "When Ally arrived, Jameela's face lit up," Zee said urgently. "And the two were inseparable the entire weekend. They stayed up late gabbing about whatever. And get this: when Ally left, she was like, 'I should come visit you guys,' and Jameela was like, 'You can stay at my house!' She hasn't even invited me to her house, and I'm her roommate!"

"That's great that Ally had a good time," Chloe said. "She probably hasn't had any good fun with her friends like that since you came to Paris."

"Yeah, she had fun here," Zee said. "But not with me."

"That's not true. You are her best friend. You've also known her since you all were super little. So she knows everything about you. Jameela is new, and they obviously hit it off. Anything new is exciting. Relax, you won't be replaced."

"I felt replaced," Zee admitted. "And exposed. Jameela also said she knew I went to therapy because she saw a notification on my computer weeks ago."

"That's strange," Chloe said. "Well, she didn't tell anyone for weeks, so why are you worried about it now?"

"I just feel like the more people know about the therapy, the more likely someone will find out and tease me about it. Or think I'm, like, the troubled kid who got sent off to boarding school."

"Not necessarily," Chloe said. "The more people know you're getting help, the more you seem on top of your issues."

Zee nodded slowly. "Since when did you get so smart and grounded all of a sudden?"

"I dunno. My two best friends are living in different countries. I guess I have time on my hands for self-improvement. So, what is up with that Archie? You guys talk much?"

"No," Zee said. "But the other day he wrote me a little song and it was so sweet. I got that butterfly feeling in my stomach again. Maybe it was a mistake to break it off with him."

"Remember that smothered feeling you used to have for that week you dated? Because he won't let you use the bathroom in peace?" Chloe said.

Zee remembered and sighed. "You're right. We should stay friends."

• • •

Zee checked her e-mail and saw that Izzy sent a link to her vlog from the weekend to Jameela and Zee. "Wow, it's up already," Zee said. She clicked open the link on her computer while Jameela looked over her shoulder.

Izzy's YouTube channel popped up and the video began to play. The title of the video appeared in Izzy's handwriting— "Sleeping and Shopping in London"—and was followed by a montage of the girls carrying their bags to the gate, hopping in the car, and laughing on the ride to Zee's house. Izzy's voice narrated as the girls rode. In the video, Zee was smiling and laughing, excited to show the girls her home, while Mrs. Carmichael was waving everyone inside.

"My mom is going to *love* seeing herself in this video," Zee said as she watched.

Izzy had recorded everything, from the gift bags to the backyard sleepover, and of course the shopping trip. She also included the girls' interactions, including happy conversations between Jameela and Ally. In the video, Zee thought they looked like old pals, giggling over jokes and singing to their favorite songs in matching pajamas. Finally, the vlog ended with footage of breakfast the next day, playing peekaboo with the twins, and goodbye hugs and kisses from Mrs. Carmichael. "Best sleepover host ever!" Izzy said in the video.

"Wow," Jameela said when it ended.

Zee nodded her head. The sleepover looked beautiful on camera. The house and Zee's family looked perfect. Izzy captured the joy of the weekend perfectly. And it seemed her fans agreed, because in just an hour it had already racked up a few thousand likes on YouTube.

"That was a fantastic weekend! I'll send the link to Ally," Jameela said, already typing away on her phone. Zee looked away from the computer screen to her. Zee wanted to send it to Ally in the Zee Files, but Jameela already beat her to it.

Zee watched the vlog a few more times, noticing how sullen her face looked as the clips went on. *Why was I unhappy that my friends were having such a good time?* She looked back at the video one more time before bed, wishing she had smiled more along the way. *We had a glamping sleepover and went shopping for dresses,* Zee thought. *Really, what was there to be sad about?*

13

MUSICAL REUNION

*A*rchie's text surprised Zee when it appeared on her phone Monday morning. She hadn't heard from him all weekend and she hadn't thought about him much, too preoccupied with the sleepover.

Archie

> **Morning, Cali. Jam session soon?**

She typed back, *Miss you*, but then deleted it. Did she really miss him?

Then she typed, *Thinking of you*. But she really hasn't. She deleted that text too.

Zee bit her lower lip, thinking of what she could write that was affectionate but true. After a minute, she came up with the only thing that felt right at the moment.

Zee

> **Good morning.**

She put her phone down on her nightstand and tried to catch a few more minutes of sleep. But the vibration of the phone wouldn't let her relax. Archie was not going to let her off without nailing down a date.

• • •

Archie was waiting for Zee in music theory class, sitting in his usual seat behind her. He watched as she sat down in front of him. "Good afternoon," he said to her.

"You're early," she replied.

"Thought we could catch up before class started. How are you? I saw you had a rocking weekend with the girls."

Zee pulled out her notes. "We had fun."

"Did you get a pretty dress for the dance?"

"Yes, Archie."

"Will I get to see it?" he asked, smiling slyly.

"Of course," Zee said. Did he remember the gang all decided to go as just friends? In any case, he would see her in the dress. "Good," he said. "Can't wait."

Mr. Hysworth walked into the classroom and kicked off the lecture. Zee turned her attention forward toward the front of the room, her pen already flowing across the page of her notebook as she took thorough notes. She wrote quickly and looked straight ahead. But those butterflies in her stomach returned, stirred up again by Archie's presence.

During the middle of class, Zee took a break from notetaking to write a short message to Archie. When Mr. Hysworth turned his back to grab more chalk, Zee quickly dropped a slip of paper on his desk: *Let's meet in practice room B after class.*

Archie smiled and wrote her a reply: *Great. Like old times, Cali. Looking forward.*

• • •

Zee and Archie met in the private practice room with new song ideas and nervous energy. They had not talked about music, much less created anything together, since the Festival.

"How's therapy going?" he asked.

"Banks said I'm crazy," Zee said.

Archie raised his eyebrows at her. "No, she didn't."

"I'm kidding," Zee said, "but she did mention something about anxiety and other problems."

"Eh, everyone's got problems."

"Yeah, but my problems are impacting my grades," Zee said.

"Just sing your way through. Teachers love that kind of creativity."

Zee looked at Archie. "You think that could work?"

Archie laughed. "I tried to serenade my English teacher at the end of last year. And I'm still making up for last year's schoolwork. So no, not so much."

Sitting near the small stage in the room, Archie swung his guitar around to rest on his thigh and started to tune it. "You know, I'm not bad on that thing either," Zee told him, nodding at the guitar.

"I didn't know you played," he said.

"It's been a while," said Zee, "with the move and adjusting to school and all. And the movers lost my guitar. Somehow it never got packed. I'm supposed to get it any day now."

"And you didn't have a fit about it?"

"They found it within a few days. It's just taking forever to get here from California."

"Right, let's see what you've got then." Archie took off his guitar and carefully placed it in Zee's hands. She grabbed the neck with one hand and pushed the body of the guitar close to her torso.

Zee started to strum the strings and sang a few lyrics that popped into her head:

"Don't know what the future holds
Time marches on both fast and slow
All we have is you and me
Wait and see
What can be..."

Archie looked at her. He felt a little spark flicker in his chest. "Wait and see, huh?"

Zee looked at him. She didn't know what she felt. She didn't know how she should feel. She liked Archie more than anyone else on campus, but she remembered what it was like to feel suffocated by him. And she remembered how judgmental he was about her friends.

"I've gotta run. I've got study group with Izzy," she said.

"Ah, right," Archie said. "I have to jet to rugby too."

Zee lifted Archie's guitar off of her and handed it back to him. Their eyes locked briefly, but she turned away quickly before she could do anything out to give him the impression they were back together. But it didn't matter. He reached over to grab the guitar, and he planted a kiss on her cheek. "See you at the dance," he said softly.

• • •

Archie walked across the quad after leaving the concert hall, happy to have spent quality time with Zee after a break. He smiled as he quickened his pace, hurrying to his rugby scrimmage with his mates. Suddenly, a slim, dark-haired girl with a heavy bag crossed his path and almost bumped into him. "Watch yourself there, ballerina," he said.

"Archie," Jameela said, looking up suddenly. "Off in a hurry?"

"Got rugby in a bit."

"I see," Jameela said. "Don't break a leg before the dance."

"You're the one who almost ran into me on the way to ballet."

"Right," Jameela said. "Speaking of the dance, are you still going with us?"

"Of course. Can't keep Zee hanging," Archie said.

"You mean, can't keep the group hanging."

"Yeah. But mainly Zee."

Jameela couldn't hide the surprise on her face. "I didn't know since you guys were broken up if you were still going. But it will be fun to hang out regardless."

Archie looked at Jameela. He didn't understand why she knew so much about his relationship, but did not want to explain anything to her. "We're not broken up. We're on a break."

At that moment, Jameela realized she had said too much. "Oh, okay, right, yes, break..."

Another awkward silence settled. Archie looked at Jameela, "Did she tell you otherwise?"

"No!" Jameela said. "I don't know anything more than you

know. And I don't know your relationship. I just... I just..."

"You just don't know what you're talking about."

Jameela looked at him nervously. "Exactly. I don't. What do I know? Um, I don't want to cause any trouble," Jameela said.

"No trouble caused," Archie said, backing away from Jameela. "I'll see you at the dance."

As he walked away, Jameela clenched her jaw, knowing she'd already said more than she should to Archie. And who knows if what she said was even right? She shook her head and took a deep breath, and hoped Archie got hit hard during his rugby match. So hard that he wouldn't remember what she said about his relationship with Zee.

Zee, who had been leaving the concert hall then, noticed across the quad Jameela and Archie talking before Archie walked off.

What was that about? Zee wondered.

14

FALL ON THE DANCE FLOOR

*T*he auditorium in the concert hall at The Hollows was decorated beautifully with autumn leaves, gold trim, and the smell of pumpkin spice in the air. Acorns and pumpkins were located all around the room, and the snacks included several variations of apple ciders, toffee breads, spicy popcorn, pretzels, and freshly baked goods available at concession stands.

Izzy had her camera rolling the entire time the gang walked across the quad from their meeting spot and toward the concert hall. She recited full fashion credits of the outfits everyone was wearing. "I don't remember who made this shirt. It's just a shirt!" Jasper said incredulously when she pressed him.

Zee, Izzy, and Jameela walked in ahead of Jasper and Tom. Archie had not yet arrived.

"Where's Archie?" Izzy asked Zee.

"Dunno," Zee replied.

"Why don't you know?" Izzy asked.

"We all are here as friends, right?" Zee said. "So he's coming alone. I don't know. He's supposed to meet us here."

"Gotcha," Izzy said. "More importantly, tell me what you're wearrrrrring..."

Zee smiled and gave a turn in her tulle frock over which she layered her coat and hand-knit scarf. "Vintage, baby! A one-of-a-kind."

"That you are, Zee," Izzy said, winking.

The group headed toward the photo booth in the near corner. Props of pumpkins, apples, and a leaf wall backdrop were set up for students to take photos with. "Ladies, we'll be here a while," Izzy declared as she instructed Jameela and Zee to pose in front of the leaf wall in various positions, both for the professional photographer manning the booth and for Izzy's own Instagram feed.

The boys took their turns in the booth, posing for a few group photos with the girls, then dispersing for the exit. "C'mon, guys, one more?" Izzy pleaded.

"No!" they said in unison. They wanted snacks. In fact, everyone wanted snacks. "Let's go to the snack bar," Zee said.

At the concession stands, the group got bags of popcorn for themselves. Zee looked around for Archie. She knew that the group had agreed to go as just friends, but she assumed he'd show up in the first couple of minutes of their arrival.

"This is my jam," Izzy said as thumping bass pumped through the speakers. "Let's dance!" She grabbed Jameela's hand and hurried off to the dance floor. Zee still had her hand in her popcorn.

"I'm going backstage to see if the band needs any help," Jasper said, shuffling off before he could be recruited to the dance floor. Tom smiled as he watched Jameela move her head back and forth and wave her hands around. Zee stood with her bag of popcorn, wondering if she would be without a dance partner all night. *Is this what I deserve after dismissing Archie as only a friend?*

Zee looked toward the entrance and froze in place. In front of her was a very, very dapper Archie wearing a perfectly fitted black sportscoat and sharply tailored pants with a perfect crease down the front of the leg. His white leather sneakers looked brand new and expensive. Archie looked directly at her and smiled. Then he started to walk toward her.

"Hi!" she said excitedly. "You clean up nicely."

"Thanks, Cali," he said. "I like this dress."

"Thank you," she said, turning in her Doc Martens to give a small twirl. "Do you want some popcorn?"

Archie smiled as he took a few kernels of popcorn from her bag. Zee smiled at him. Jameela and Izzy waved to him from the dance floor and came closer. "You missed the photo shoot in the booth!" Izzy said.

"My bad," Archie said, putting his hand on his chest.

Zee turned to Archie. "Maybe you and I can do a shoot later by ourselves?"

"Let's go somewhere and talk about that. Shall we?" Archie said.

Zee looked at him carefully. "Sure."

The two took a seat at a corner table of the concert hall and looked at the crowd gathered on the dance floor. "Band's great, yeah?" Archie said.

"Yeah, they're pretty great," Zee agreed. "I think they've been performing at Moe's mostly."

"I wouldn't know," said Archie. "I haven't been to Moe's since we last went there together."

"Aww, Archie, don't let me keep you from those turmeric lattes."

"Right," Archie said.

Zee nudged his knee with hers. "I miss you."

"Not what I heard," Archie said.

"What do you mean?"

"Word on the street is we broke up."

"Well, we did. Sort of." Zee thought back to what Dr. Banks had told her about trying to become friends with Archie. She looked at Archie. "Look, it's not like I don't want to be with you. I do, but maybe we should... take things slower? There's no need for us to be in a relationship for us to hang out together."

"But I don't just want to be your friend like Jasper is your friend," Archie said. "We have something special. Something different."

"What's wrong with how Jasper is my friend?" Zee asked.

"Nothing, but I don't want to be Jasper."

"Okay, I don't understand. What's so bad about Jasper?"

"As a human being? Nothing. But you and I are different."

Zee turned her head sharply. "Why do we need to make things so different? I'm different enough!" Zee said.

"It establishes boundaries," Archie said.

"I'm an inclusive person, Archie. Boundaries aren't my thing." Zee shook her head. "I think it's best if we are just friends without the labels. I think the labels are what's making things weird."

Archie put his head in his hands and rubbed his face. "So, are we done?"

"No, that is not what I'm saying. I just think that we should be friends. I'm really just getting adjusted here in the U.K. I've got therapy, the paper—I've got a lot going on right now."

As he studied her face, Archie realized he could no longer fight to keep Zee all to himself. If he did, he may lose her completely. "All right, Cali. I understand."

"Nothing has to change, Archie. I still want to hang out with you. I still want to make music with you. But maybe having fewer rules and labels will make things easier."

"I understand."

"Okay," Zee said. "Shall we try it out over this dance?"

"I don't dance," Archie said.

"Oh, come on, just one dance?"

Archie looked at Zee. Her eyes twinkled under the disco lights as she tilted her head to the side. That sunny, California charm of Zee's won every time. "All right," he said. He grabbed Zee's hand and reluctantly shuffled behind her to the dance floor.

• • •

Jameela had not danced on her feet in regular shoes to pop music in months. Any time she danced, it was for ballet. It felt refreshing to be off her toes.

"Looking good there. Kept your balance and everything," Tom said, watching her from the sidelines.

"That song was in fact my jam," she said. "Why haven't I seen you dancing?"

"I guess because no one has asked me to dance yet."

"What?" Jameela responded. "I was waiting for you to join me."

"Well, how was I supposed to know that?"

"By my eyes!" Jameela said. "I totally gave you the 'go ahead' eyes."

"The 'go ahead' eyes?"

"Yes, the 'go ahead and ask me to dance' eyes."

"Say what?"

"These," Jameela said. She moved her top eyelids up and down, winking but also looking more like she was imitating a car hood closing halfway down on a car. "This is my come-hither look."

Tom laughed. "I don't want to get anywhere near whatever is going on with your eyes there. You look like you've got a fly in there or something."

"You don't know flirting when you see it."

"No, I'm just not seeing it. So, I'll just be direct—would like to dance?"

Jameela stopped half-blinking her eyes and put her hands on her hips. Then she stuck one of her hands out toward him. "Fine. But I'll lead."

• • •

"We're here LIIIIIVVEEEE at the Harvest Dance, whooooo!" Izzy said into her phone as she recorded footage of the concert hall packed with students, bopping and dancing to the music. "This is the. Place. To. Be. On. A Friday. Night!"

Izzy ran toward the dance floor with her phone in hand, Poppy following closely behind her. The two shimmied to the thumping beat from the speakers and pointed their fingers in the air, to the sides and down, and at anyone who was looking at them. "Yass, Poppy!" Izzy said, excited for the dance vibes.

Zee was still dancing with Archie—one song became two, and now to a number neither of them could recall. Izzy smiled as she watched them move, her camera phone still recording. Then Izzy caught Jameela and Tom just a few paces away, dancing to their own rhythm. Zee also glanced toward Jameela. *Is Jameela actually having a good ol' time?* Zee wondered. She had never seen her roommate so carefree.

Then Zee looked over at the other side of the room and saw Jasper. He was alone, a bag of popcorn in his hand after losing track of his friends. He looked toward the dance floor, and in an instant his eyes locked with Zee. Zee tried to create some distance between her and Archie. She wanted to make space for Jasper on the dance floor.

"Jassy! Get over here!" Izzy cried out. She lunged herself toward Jasper, grabbing him by the arm and pulling him. Zee slowly stopped dancing, pausing long enough for Archie to notice what had distracted her. Jasper and Izzy grooved together and Izzy wrapped her arm around his neck and put the camera in front of their faces. "My dance partner for life! Whoooo!" she declared into the camera.

Zee looked over and felt a pang of jealousy at Jasper dancing with Izzy. It only lasted for a second. But as her eyes took in everyone on the dance floor, she realized she was among friends. Good friends. New friends. And there they were together, all of them, her talented, zany, and loving friends at The Hollows Creative Arts Academy.

Maybe I'm more at home than I thought, Zee thought to herself.

15

A TRICKY ASSIGNMENT

By Saturday afternoon, the Zee Files was still lacking photos and videos from the Harvest Dance. Chloe started a group text between Zee and Ally to see what happened.

Chloe

Well????????

Zee

Well, what?

Chloe

Well, how was the dance?

Zee

It was okay.

Chloe

OKAY?! Not one photo of you and Archie together? Not even one of you in your dress? Not buying it. Conference call immediately.

A few minutes later, Zee, Ally, and Chloe were on a video call. Chloe's face looked unimpressed at Zee's answers. Ally's face was curious and inquisitive, like a reporter at a political press conference.

"So you broke up with him. For good?" Chloe asked.

Zee sighed loudly. "Did I make a big mistake?"

"How do you feel this morning?" Chloe asked.

"I got my best night of sleep in days."

"Well, there's your answer."

Zee nodded. "I just feel so bad."

"Why? You said you'd be friends, you didn't tell him to jump in a lake. It's fine. He's a big boy," Ally said.

"Agreed," Chloe said. "He'll be fine. He'll buy some new sneakers, or a new guitar, or someone else's prized possession. And nothing lasts forever. Maybe later you'll get back together."

"Did you have one final kiss?" Ally asked.

"We did kiss," Zee said. "But like Chloe said, who said it had to be final?"

Ally nodded. "True, things could change. Maybe when more time passes you can revisit. So what happens now?"

"I go to class. On time. Without a chaperone. I have more time to write. I eat meals with Jameela and Tom and Jasper again, uninterrupted. I drink my turmeric lattes alone," Zee answered.

"These sound like song lyrics," Chloe said.

"Well, my life is a song," Zee said.

"Oh dear," Chloe said.

"What? Where is the lie there?"

Chloe giggled as she scrolled through her phone. She looked at other photos from that evening. "But for real, you think you could use this as fodder for one of your English papers or something?"

Something clicked in Zee's mind. "Oh, that reminds me, Ella from the paper left a message for me. I should get back to her. Maybe it's another assignment. I'll keep you both posted on what happens," she said.

After hanging up with Chloe and Ally, Zee called Ella, who picked up immediately. "Hey, Zee! Thanks for calling. Did you have fun at the Harvest Dance?"

"Yeah, it was great! Cool music, huh?"

"Yeah, the band was awesome," Ella said. "Listen, I wanted to assign you another story for the paper. The other staffers really liked how you treated the Izzy piece. It also got really great traffic online. Her social following certainly helped, but a lot of her traffic came from local readers too."

"Oh, cool!" Zee said. "I'd love to do another story. Is there someone you had in mind for me to interview?"

"Actually, yes," Ella said. "Archie Saint John."

Zee held her breath while she processed what Ella just said. *Could the timing be any worse?* she thought to herself.

"Archie?" Zee responded. "Why?"

"Because he's the most interesting and mysterious person on campus. No one knows much about him. Besides you, that is, being his girlfriend and all."

"Ex-girlfriend," Zee said. "I mean, good friend."

"Ex? You two didn't look like exes at the Harvest Dance. You two were dancing and talking together all night."

"How do you know that? Were you spying on me?"

"No, but it was hard to miss you two. I mean, wherever Archie goes, he draws attention."

Zee had a sneaking feeling that the only reason Ella asked her to contribute to the paper was to get info on Archie. But she didn't know why. "What do you want the interview to be about?"

"Just asking him the basic stuff. Where he's from, what he likes, favorite subjects, favorite hobbies, life goals, family stuff. We'll write it as if the campus is just meeting him for the first time."

"But he was at The Hollows last year," Zee said.

"Yeah, but he's never around and has very few friends. So no one knows him."

Zee thought about what it would be like to write about her ex-boyfriend. Could she put enough space between herself and the subject to write the story objectively? *I wrote about Izzy objectively, and she is one of my good friends,* Zee thought.

"I have to think about this one," Zee said. "Can I get back to you?"

"Okay, but don't think too long. We have a deadline coming," Ella said. Zee nodded even though she knew Ella couldn't see her, and hung up.

• • •

Zee and Jasper sat across from each other in sciences. Their oceans project was due next week, though they had not had the time to work on it between the Harvest Dance and other distractions.

"We gotta hustle to get this together," Zee said. "Can we focus on this in our study group?"

"We can, but I think we'll also need to get our handouts

for our presentation. We'll need another time to go to the printers," Jasper pointed out.

"Okay, fine."

"Is it fine, Zee? You'll have the time between school and Archie?"

"Archie and I are just friends now, Jasper," Zee said, annoyed. "We only hang out occasionally. I have the time."

Jasper looked at Zee. "Good."

"Good?"

"Yeah, good," said Jasper.

"Good, as in it's good I'm not with Archie?"

"Good, as in you'll have time for this project—but since you asked, yes, it was good you broke up with him," said Jasper. "He's not a good influence, Zee. He's behind in school,

he's never here, he only cares about himself, and the more time you spent with him, the worse off you would have been."

Zee looked at him. "You mean the guy wrote me several songs and spent more time with me than you have, even though we've known each other longer."

"He stole your time, Zee. Much different," Jasper said. "Anyway, now that you're free, I look forward to spending more time hanging out and working on this project."

"Fantastic. Me too," Zee said sarcastically.

Jasper gathered his books, shoved them into his backpack, and hurried out of class. Zee slumped back in her seat, exasperated at yet another tiff with Jasper over Archie. Then she sat up and decided to go back to her room for a little break before her late morning classes.

• • •

Kicking her shoes off at the door, Zee plopped herself on her bed, allowing her backpack to fall behind her. She took a deep breath. Surely she can figure this Archie friendship out. And this Jasper one, which seemed to be just as complicated. She took out her computer and went to the one place where she knew she'd find the answer to resolving both relationships.

Pulling up her web browser, she found the Google homepage. In the search bar, she typed: *Can girls and boys be just friends?*

The results: too many to count.

16

PASSING ON A STORY

*I*t was the first day in a long time that Zee did not see Archie sitting in his usual seat behind her in music theory class. She had mixed emotions about his absence—she was relieved so she could focus on the lecture the entire time, but she also missed the challenge of taking notes while he tried to distract her with his smile or his flirty behavior.

After class, Zee texted him: *Hey! Where were you today?*

She walked with her phone in hand as she meandered across the quad. Zee hadn't seen Archie all day today. Actually, she hadn't seen him since the Harvest Dance.

A few minutes later, her phone buzzed.

Archie

> Hey. I'm in London. Came home for a few days. Lying low.

Zee

> Oh, okay. You want my notes from art theory this week?

Archie

Nah, I'm good. Text you when I'm back.

Zee felt like Archie was preoccupied. She tried once more to get his attention.

Zee

You sure? I can bring you whatever you need. Turmeric latte? California sunshine?

Archie

I'll pass. Thanks.

• • •

Though she held staff meetings every Monday and Wednesday at 3:30 p.m. for students to pitch stories and turn in assignments, Ella spent every weekday afternoon at the headquarters of *The Hollows Post* to oversee coverage of all the fall happenings on campus, including the Creative Arts Festival and the Harvest Dance. News moved fast near the holidays, which she was quite happy about.

Zee went to *The Hollows Post* newsroom to meet Ella and give her the decision about writing a story on Archie. Zee had thought long and hard about it—in the shower, during class, even while standing in line for that vegan shepherd's pie dinner special a few nights back. She wrote about her decision-making process in her journal and created a lengthy pros and cons list. She wrote all the reasons it would be fun to do (*it's easy; because I know the subject; he's interesting; he'd talk to me*) and all the reasons not to do it (*it would be awkward; he might say no; I don't want him to think we're back together; interviewing an ex-boyfriend is hard and weird*). In the end, she had five pros and sixteen cons.

Wondering if maybe she was overthinking the Archie story, Zee asked Jameela what she thought ("Interviewing your ex-boyfriend for the paper? Super awkward.") and what her therapist, Dr. Banks, thought ("I agree with Jameela, Zee."). By Wednesday afternoon, Zee made her decision. And she felt good about it, no matter how Ella might feel about it.

Zee walked into the room and saw a few students typing at computers and two English teachers gathered with Ella, discussing the paper's layout. Ella gave a wave to Zee from across the room and held one finger up. Zee sat on the couch and flipped through the most recent edition of the paper.

A few minutes later, Ella appeared next to her. "Sorry about that. Mrs. Pender and Mr. Glass are the advisors for the paper and were giving me some information about a promotion they want to run in the next issue."

"No worries," Zee said. "I have Mrs. Pender for English lit."

"Yeah? Her class is tough! But it got me interested in the paper after we studied a few famous newspaper editorials in class last year."

"I wonder if I'll have that same creative spark in her class," Zee said. "So far there's just a lot of anxiety over my essays."

"It gets better toward the end of the year," Ella said. "Anyway, what's up?"

"I just wanted to come by in person to tell you what I decided about the Archie piece," Zee said. She took a breath and sat up straighter. "I just can't do it right now. For one, it's just... I don't think he's reachable right now. And two, I'm a bit tied up with schoolwork this week to get it done."

Ella looked disappointed. "Really? I thought you could reach him at any time. You're his girlfriend—I mean, ex-girlfriend!"

"Yeah, I can text him, but I can't sit down for an interview with him right now."

"Then do the interview via text," Ella said persistently. "Or e-mail the questions and he can get back to you when he's free."

Zee felt uneasy by how strong Ella pushed back on her. "I tried texting him this morning and I didn't get a response. And this week I have a big sciences project due. I can't spend tons of time chasing him down."

"Yeah, but that's why you can e-mail him. He can respond to you even while you're studying. And then you can get the story done after you turn in your project. Shall we say Monday for the deadline then?"

Zee could feel the anxiety building in her belly. She tried to be polite with Ella, but now she'd have to be stern. "Listen, a story on Archie isn't happening right now. Assign me someone else."

Ella looked at her with a slight frown on her face. She placed her hands in her lap and sat upright. "Zee, if there's no Archie, then I have no other assignment right now. I gave you the first two assignments for the paper to get you involved, but if you can't execute half of those, then maybe you don't want to be a part of the paper after all."

"I do want to be a part of the paper," Zee said. "I just can't report on my ex-boyfriend right now! Can't you understand that?"

Ella pursed her lips. "Why don't you come back when you have the time then, yeah?"

She stood up from her chair and flounced off.

Zee felt as if she just got dumped. She gathered her copy of the paper and quietly left the office, not knowing if she'd ever be invited back to return.

• • •

Zee walked back to her dorm, her stomach queasy from the conversation with Ella. The anxiety over the thought of interviewing her ex-boyfriend had been replaced by the uneasiness over disappointing the editor of the school newspaper. As she passed by the common area of the dorm, she saw a few girls who lived on the first floor gathered to watch television. Another group of girls were batting a ball around the ping-pong table. Zee thought about joining either group, but then remembered her oceans project.

As she made her way to the second floor and to her dorm room, Izzy rounded the corner and ran into her. "Hey, Zee! You done for the day?"

"Jasper and I have to work on this oceans project. You off to soccer?"

"Yeah, a little scrimmage at the park. This may be the last day we can play outside. It's so cold out around now. And it gets dark so early. Is that the paper?" Izzy asked.

"Oh, yeah," Zee said, forgetting she was still carrying the issue under her arm.

"My mum loved your story on me! Got any other stories coming up?"

"Well, Ella asked me to write something on Archie, but I just declined."

"Ella just asked you to write about Archie?" Izzy made a face. "That's so weird."

"I know, right? I don't want to write about my ex. Ella keeps asking me a lot of questions about Archie. It's a bit uncomfortable."

"Yeah, I can imagine why," Izzy said. "She had the biggest crush on him last year."

Zee blinked a few times. "No! I didn't know that."

"She threw herself at him constantly. Even took over the school newspaper thinking she could get closer to him by getting an interview with him. But he wasn't interested, much less ever around."

Zee looked at Izzy. "This makes so much more sense."

"Yeah?"

"I told Ella I wasn't comfortable with doing a story on

Archie right now and she acted like I insulted her mother."

"Probably because she was jealous and then upset that her plan to get closer to Archie again wouldn't work," Izzy said. "Sorry, Ella!"

- "Unbelievable," Zee said.

"At least you realized this now before you wrote and reported a whole story on your ex-boyfriend. That would have been super weird."

"So true," Zee said. "So true."

"Have you spoken to him since the dance?"

"A brief text message, but no, not really."

"Hmm," Izzy said. "Watch out for Ella. She likes drama, she likes Archie, and getting you to write about Archie gets her drama and scoop on him. You have enough going on in your life already."

• • •

After a quick dinner, Zee went back to her dorm room. She peeled off her school uniform and changed into her pajamas, then crawled into bed to get some studying done.

Zee still felt uneasy about Ella's pressure to write about Archie. She closed her eyes and breathed deeply, and tried to think about something else as a distraction. But nothing worked. Finally, she took out her journal where she kept the writing prompts from Dr. Banks. One of them said: *What was something today that challenged you, and what did you learn about yourself from it?*

The question made Zee pause. She began writing the words down in her journal, her handwriting slanting to the right as if she could not get the words down on the page fast enough.

The most challenging thing of my day was dealing with Ella pressuring me to write a piece about my ex-boyfriend. I felt uneasy with the assignment, and then uncomfortable about how much she was pressuring me to do it even after I told her how I felt. It made me not want to write for the paper again.

Then she thought about the second part of the prompt. *What did I learn about myself?* She thought about what Izzy told her about Ella, about Ella's strategy to get closer to Archie. Zee thought about how she did not buckle under the pressure from Ella to do the story. About how Ella didn't have compassion toward Zee. *I feel bad for Ella,* she thought, *but I would have felt worse if I would have had to interview my ex-boyfriend.*

Zee started to write in her journal.

I learned that I am pretty strong in the face of peer pressure. Even when Ella pushed me to the story on Archie, I still told her no. I wasn't going to be bullied into the piece.

Zee smiled as she closed her journal and let out a long exhale. Her stomach stopped hurting and her headache subsided. Feeling a weight lift off her chest, Zee turned over to place the journal in her bedside nightstand drawer, turned off the light, and leaned back on her pillow, falling asleep a few minutes later.

17

CALIFORNIA BREAK

The air in the English countryside got cooler and crisper each morning. The trees on campus had become barer each week, most of their leaves already fallen and either swept away or crunched into small bits from the footsteps of Hollows students. The sky took more time to turn to light each morning, and with each passing day it took Zee even more time to rise and shine.

The changing seasons meant the campus was creeping closer to winter break, and while there were still a few weeks left in the semester, Zee was already looking forward to what the winter would bring. It would be her first winter spent in a cold climate for more than a few days. She looked forward to things like snow, roasted marshmallows, and the smell of pine and peppermint in the air.

Zee's phone buzzed on a late afternoon after a day of classes. It was her mother calling.

"Hi, darling!" Mrs. Carmichael chirped. "How are you?"

"I'm all right. Is something up?" Zee asked.

"No, darling just wanted to hear your voice."

"Really? How are the twins?"

"Amazing. Growing like weeds. Asking for you all the time."

"Ahh, I miss them."

"Well, darling, lucky for you we will all be together for the winter break," said Mrs. Carmichael. "That's really why I'm calling. I wanted to tell you that we are going back to California for break. All of us—even your big brother is coming back from university. Surprise!"

Zee took the largest inhale her lungs could hold. "REAAALLLLYYY?! Oh. My. Lanta, that's amazing!"

"I figured you'd be excited," Mrs. Carmichael said. "We rented a house in Malibu so we can be near the beach."

"Oh, this is going to be the most amazing holiday ever!" Zee said eagerly. "Malibu! Together! Can Chloe come? Pleeeeeeaaaaaaaase?"

"I'm not sure what the Johnsons' plans are, but we will be in a beautiful beachfront home. With Camilla, obviously."

Zee's smile fell. "Camilla's coming? On our family vacation?"

"We will need someone to take care of the twins," Mrs. Carmichael said.

"But wouldn't you do that?"

"Of course, but I can use the extra hand. Besides, I'm more concerned about you. Your father and I figured you could use this trip more than anything. You know, give you a little taste of home for the holidays."

Zee sat up in her bed and looked at her nightstand. There was a photo of her with The Beans from one of her last school performances, and a photo of her, Chloe, and Ally together at her old house. Zee had created some fun new memories at The Hollows, no doubt, but she missed the good ol' days at Brookdale.

"I'm so excited! I can't wait to get home. Where's the house exactly? Can you send me pictures? How did you find it?" Zee asked her mother.

"Instagram!" her mother raved.

An amused smile formed on Zee's face. "Naturally."

• • •

Guess who's coming back to Cali!!! Zee texted Chloe right after having talked with her mom. Zee was already envisioning herself by the pool with Chloe in matching red one-piece bathing suits. She couldn't wait for a whole three weeks of vacation by the beach with her friends where she could just relax.

Chloe called back immediately. "GET. OUT!" she said. "The whole time?"

"Yes!"

"In Malibu?"

"YES! A reunion! I told you I wouldn't be gone for that long."

"Whoooo!" Chloe said. "This is going to be the best holiday ever!"

"Let's start making plans now for it so we can align our schedules," Zee said. "I am so craving those peppermint smoothies from Bucks."

"I know, and we've to get those gingerbread muffins too. We'll need, like, a dozen!"

"And we'll have to get matching pajamas so we can do a

photo shoot. And then have, like, eight sleepovers. Or one weeklong sleepover!"

"I know!" Chloe said. "That would be easier on my parents anyway. Why drive from L.A. to Malibu for just a day or two? That traffic is not worth a day trip. I *have* to stay all week."

Zee laughed. "And I can come and stay at your house too! I wonder if we can get the band back there again?"

"Like, to perform?"

"Well, maybe not, but at least to hang out. I haven't heard from Landon or that dreadful Kathi in so long. Oh, and Mr. P.! Maybe a quick reunion with the gang."

"Could be fun!" Chloe enthused. "Everyone is still the same. Landon is still Landon. Kathi is still Kathi, though slightly less annoying and spiteful since you left. I think—and I can't believe I'm saying this—she misses you."

Zee nearly dropped her phone. Kathi Barney was her frenemy back at Brookdale Academy. She was pretty and popular, but was only nice to people when she needed something from them. "Excuse me, I think I misheard you. Did you say Kathi missed me?" Zee asked.

"The other day we ran into each other in the hallway and she asked about you. Said it's weird not seeing you around school."

"I never thought Kathi would miss me. It's like pigs are flying in the air."

"Big pigs! Anyway, this is the best news ever!" Chloe said. "Let me tell my parents right away so we can work out our schedules. I can't wait to see you!"

• • •

Skills for Life's last major project was a Sunday roast for the entire class. It was a family-style meal in class that included techniques and dishes they had learned to cook over the past few weeks, and was also a lovely way to toast to their hard work during the semester. As a pair, Tom and Zee were assigned a few sautéed vegetable dishes for their last class.

"Any plans for the holiday?" Tom asked Zee as he seasoned some asparagus spears.

"Actually, yes! My mom texted me yesterday and said we're going back to California for the break," Zee told him.

"Ah, right on," Tom said. "That's brilliant. It'll be nice to see your old friends and favorite places to hang out."

"Yeah, I'm excited. What about you?"

"My mum's coming back from some project in Mumbai that she was on for the past couple weeks, so we're actually

staying local. I really like holidays in London," Tom said as he cracked some black pepper over the greens.

"I'm sure. Actual snow. I haven't seen it in a long time," Zee said. "I think Jameela is staying here too."

Tom looked over at Jameela standing at another cooking station. "So I hear," Tom said.

Zee looked curiously at Tom. "So, like, what's up with you two?"

"Nothing's up," Tom said. "She's... a project."

"A project?" Zee said. "What, like an old car?"

"No! She's, like... We've known each other since we were super young, and she's changed. Like, for the better. And this better Jameela is more fun to hang with."

"Yeah, she's not so..."

"Uptight?" Tom guessed.

"Exactly."

"Right."

"So maybe you two could hang out and do some yoga or something during break," Zee suggested.

"Maybe," Tom said. "But yoga is really a personal practice. Something one often does alone. Maybe we'll have a proper meetup."

Mrs. Templeton stood in front of the classroom where the long communal table was set up for tastings. The students carefully placed their finished meals around the table, which included a beautiful roast beef, Yorkshire puddings, shepherd's pie, and roasted vegetables. "Let's get started," Mrs. Templeton said. "Everything smells so delicious!"

Jameela took a seat on the other side of Tom and Zee, and Izzy and Jasper sat next to them. Each pair of students briefly described how they cooked their dish and what they liked about it while Mrs. Templeton took notes and assessed their meals. Then everyone dug into their plates full of food. Laughter and clanging of dishes echoed throughout the class.

Chewing on the asparagus she had cooked, Zee looked around the room and felt a sense of ease. After a challenging semester at The Hollows, comfort in at least one of her classes had finally come in the form of her friends at the table, delicious food, and the stellar marks she and Tom received for their work in Skills for Life.

18

DREAMING OF HOME

The last of Zee's classes went by in a flash. Algebra class ended with an exam covering the last four chapters of the textbook, which Zee did her best to study for. She went over notes with Izzy and Jasper during their study group and asked lots of questions. The night before the exam, Zee even listened to one of the meditations Jameela had showed her earlier—and Zee actually stayed awake long enough to follow the entire thing. During the exam, she worked hard to focus on the equations on the page. She only daydreamed once about California, then the holidays, then who invented Santa. When she received her grades back, she got a solid above-average mark. And she was happy.

For sciences, Jasper helped Zee organize her notes and outline the visuals for their oceans project. The two presented their oceans fundraising idea for Mr. Roth class the day after the algebra final, and Mr. Roth approved. "I think we should actually do this," he said. "Would you two be interested in organizing it during Earth Day in the spring?" They both received high marks for the presentation, boosting Zee's grade up to above average.

English lit also ended on a high note. Mrs. Pender gave Zee the option to write a song for her Shakespeare assignment instead of a traditional essay. From there, Zee became way more engaged in class. She finished the reading and composed a short song around a theme from *Macbeth*. Eager to bring it back to the classroom, Zee performed it in front of everyone without angst. Mrs. Pender was pleasantly impressed. "Well done, Zee. Very well done," she said.

Intro to art history and music theory also finished smoothly. Archie didn't show up for the rest of the classes, as he had mentioned to Zee, so her concentration remained on her notes and Mr. Hysworth's lecture the entire time. She got a high mark with little effort. *Music is just my jam*, she thought to herself.

In the middle of the week, Zee also had her last visit to Dr. Banks before the break. Dr. Banks had a full legal pad of notes from their near two months' worth of meetings. Her face softened as Zee sat down in front of her.

"So, Zee, what's going on?" Dr. Banks asked. "Lots has happened these past few weeks. How are you feeling now?"

"I feel..." Zee said, searching her body for sensations like nervousness or anxiousness. She just felt relaxed. "Okay. I feel all right now."

"How are your classes finishing up?"

"I think they're going to be okay. Algebra ended with me getting a passing grade, so that's better than a failing one."

"Did you really think you'd fail?"

"It wasn't looking too good there for a while."

Dr. Banks chuckled. "What about Mrs. Pender's class? English literature. Did that end okay?"

"She said I could write a song for my Shakespeare assignment and I rocked it!"

"You rocked it?"

"Since I could sing the assignment, I had more fun with it. Way easier to sing it."

"For you, yes," Dr. Banks said. "If it were me, I could never! I know we've been talking about ADHD a bit lately, but that's an example of how someone with ADHD can work with their strengths to overcome homework—or any challenge, really. It doesn't have to be something that's debilitating if you can recognize what your strengths are and work with those."

"Right," Zee said. "If only I could sing about algebra equations instead."

"Try it sometime, you never know," Dr. Banks said. "And have you been journaling or doing any of the exercises we've talked about?"

"A few, yes."

"Have they been helping?"

"Sometimes."

"Keep trying them out. I can send you more prompts if you need," Dr. Banks said. "So, things seem good?"

Zee looked at her hands. They were lying still in her lap. Her feet relaxed on the floor. "Yeah, for now. I mean, we're about to go away on break. Finals are pretty much done. I have a trip home to look forward to, so I'm pretty excited."

Dr. Banks smiled. "Indeed you are. You've made a lot of progress this semester, Zee. I'm proud of you."

"Thanks, Dr. Banks," Zee said. "Until next semester?"

"Yes, Zee. Reach out any time you need me on e-mail. Have fun in California."

· · ·

Just as Zee walked out of Dr. Banks's office, her phone vibrated in her backpack. She fished it out and saw it was a text from Archie.

Archie

> Hey, Cali.

Zee

> It's been a minute. Have you gone MIA again?

Archie

> No. Still in London. At this point since we're so close to break, I finished up my classes online. Teachers were cool with it. Probably won't be back until after the holidays.

Zee felt a ping of sadness knowing that she wouldn't see Archie for the rest of the semester.

Zee

> Wow, and you didn't even say goodbye.

Archie

> I'd never say goodbye to you, Cali. Only see you later.

Zee blushed. She felt that flutter in her heart again.

Zee

> Aww, in this case, see you next year.

Archie

> Indeed. What are you doing for the holiday?

Zee

> Heading back to Cali.

Archie

> Wow. Send me a postcard.

Zee

> I'll save the money for stamps and send you a photo. You need to see the Malibu sunsets. Will warm your chilly holiday evenings.

Archie

> Perfect, Cali. Miss you.

And with that, Zee felt some closure to her relationship with Archie Saint John. A sense of normalcy had returned between them. Flirty texts, no sense of when exactly they'd see each other next—Zee felt surprising comfort in that sort of unknown. She shook her head, tossed her phone back into her backpack, and made her way toward the dorm.

• • •

Photos of the Malibu holiday house from Mrs. Carmichael came into Zee's inbox quickly. The first ones were of the living room, with oversized white sectionals and fluffy pillows, and large wood tables. Then photos of the kitchen revealed countertops large enough to dance on, the white marble making the perfect backdrop for Instagram cooking videos. The bedrooms, all eight of them, were huge and sun drenched. The den, a movie theater, and a trampoline in the backyard just beyond the pool all looked like a dreamy oasis. *This is paradise,* Zee thought. *And in a few short weeks, it will be my paradise.*

"Honey, it's amazing," her mother told Zee on the phone. "And because you felt a bit slighted about your room in London, why don't you pick your room now, before everyone else has a chance to?"

"Yes!" Zee said as she browsed through the pictures. "This is large enough for any sleepover. Chloe can come and visit us for a few nights, right?"

"Of course," Mrs. Carmichael said. "Is Ally going to be in town?"

"I don't know. But wouldn't that be awesome if she could come too?"

"We have plenty of room," Mrs. Carmichael said. "Ask and see what she says. Oh, one other thing, your guitar finally arrived here at the house."

Zee gasped. "Finally! I've been dying to play again." Her excitement for the holiday break grew even more. "Can't wait to head home."

Zee grabbed her large suitcase from under her bed and opened it on the floor space between her and Jameela's beds. Zee would not leave the dorm for another two days, but she didn't want to wait until the last minute. *Wow, I'm actually early on this bit of homework*, she thought to herself.

She placed her favorite sweatshirts and leggings inside the suitcase, followed by her T-shirts and dresses. She left the whole other side of the suitcase for dirty clothes. She would gather the last of her belongings tomorrow afternoon before she left campus.

She placed her journal on top of the stack of clean clothes, and her music journal on top of the writing journal. Just as she took a step back from her suitcase, her phone rang.

"Hey, Zee, what's up?" Ally said through the receiver.

"Ally! I'm packing up for holiday."

"Already?"

"We're leaving in a few days. Might as well start now," Zee said. "Did I tell you where I'm going? Oh my gosh, I might have been too caught up with finals. We're going to Malibu! Whoo whoo!"

"Get. Out!" Ally said. "That's so fun!"

"Yeah, my mom told me the other day. I can't believe it. I mean, I thought we were going to have our first holiday here, but we can get some snow here first and then head west for warm weather."

"That's awesome," Ally said. "Is Chloe so excited? I'm jealous. I wish I were going."

"What are you doing for the break?" Zee asked.

"I'm staying with my dad," Ally said. "He's got some big article due for the *Times*, so we'll be here while he finishes. My mom is going back to Cali though. I think she's staying with my aunt."

"Are you happy about spending the break in Paris? Is that what you did last year?"

"Yeah," Ally said. "Paris during that time is great. But my parents arguing was what I remember most from last year."

"Can't you go with your mom back to California? Then we can all be together this year! I'm sure you could even stay with us. My mom showed me pictures of the house. It's ridiculous!"

"I'd love to, but I think my dad will be crushed if I leave him here alone."

"Or will he? Maybe he wants to work. Can you ask him? Oh, please, pretty please!" Zee pleaded.

Ally paused for a second. "Sure, I'll ask my dad, but don't hold your breath."

"Yesss!"

"Really, Zee, don't hold your breath!"

"Too late!" Zee pretended to gasp for air.

"Zee!" Ally laughed. "I'll ask!"

Zee could hardly wait. "Call him now! Then call me back!"

Zee plopped down on her bed, her mind buzzing with thoughts about the break. About no more algebra, or Mrs. Pender, or sciences. About gingerbread, and hot chocolates, and peppermint-flavored candies. About the beach and riding bikes outside in Malibu. And that trampoline at that house. "Going back to Caliiiiii!" she squealed to herself.

An hour later, Jameela walked into their room with her ballet leotard under a peacoat and riding boots. She left her overcoat and boots at the door and greeted Zee. "Hi there. Had a late practice that ran through dinner. All packed up for

California? That will be quite the break."

"Yeah! I'm super excited. Beach, warm weather, ocean... old friends."

"Right. You're practically beaming right now."

"What are you doing for break?" Zee asked Jameela.

"Ms. Duckett is working throughout the break, so she expects me at practices too."

"So you have to be at school the whole time?"

"Oh no," Jameela said. "She happens to have a studio near my house, so on school breaks she teaches from there. No rest for me."

"I'm sorry," Zee said.

"It's fine. It gives me something to do. Better than sitting at home for two weeks." Jameela sat down on her bed. "Tom asked if we could hang out during break. Says he'll be in London."

"Ooh, that sounds *innnnn*-teresting!" Zee said.

"Calm down, we're just old friends," Jameela said. "We've known each other forever."

"Right," Zee said.

"Anyway, you ready for home?"

"Yes, indeed! I can't wait."

"Cool, Zee. Hope you don't stay there forever. I'd miss you."

Zee cleared her throat and put her hand to her collarbone. "I'm sorry, I must have heard something wrong. Did you say you'd miss me?"

"Don't be such a drama queen," said Jameela. "Yes, I'll miss you. Say hi to Ally for me."

"Ally?" Zee said. "How do you know I invited her to California?"

"I, um... I have to brush my teeth," Jameela said, and dashed out of the room.

Zee watched her roommate leave. Why would Jameela have known that? Was she still talking to Ally since the sleepover?

• • •

Once Zee finished packing what she could for the evening, she changed into her pajamas, brushed her teeth and washed her face, cleaned up the last few bits of clothes and books scattered around her side of the room, and crawled into bed. Her body was tired from everything the school year had thrown at her so far. New friends. A relationship. A talent show. Finals. And now, a trip back home to California. Zee's mind was spinning, and to calm it, she planned on listening to one of her meditations from that app Jameela turned her on to.

When Zee pulled up the meditation app on her phone, a call from Ally came in. "Guess what?!" Ally said breathlessly.

"What?" Zee sat up in bed.

"My mom said I could come to L.A. with her. And just like you said, Dad is on deadline and he agreed to let me go there right after school lets out."

"Are you serious? You're coming?!"

"Yup! Our moms are working out the flights and stuff now!"

"GET. OUT!" Zee said loudly. The reality sunk into Zee's mind. Her best friend was coming back to California with her for a week, and they were going to reunite with their whole Brookdale crew, including their other BFF. No Zoom calls needed. No texts, because they'd be together in person. "Like, seriously?"

"I know, right? I am so happy. I think your mom called up my dad to convince him to let me go. But yeah, looks like the whole gang will be back together again. I'm so excited."

"That's the best gift I could have ever received!" Zee said. "California, here we come!"

"I'm stoked. Let's talk tomorrow about schedules. Can't wait to see you!" Ally said.

Zee put down her phone on her bedstand. She was so excited about what was in store in the next few weeks. Her three best friends together with her family, just like old times.

"Eekkk!" she said excitedly, kicking the covers underneath the sheet. Jameela walked back into the room.

"What's up?" Jameela asked.

"Wait," Zee said and looked at her. "Did you know Ally was coming to Cali before me? You did, didn't you."

"We were texting about shopping, and then her dad came in and said she could go," Jameela said. "She told me she was calling you."

"I can't believe... oh, never mind. I'm just so excited."

"You'll have so much fun. Take tons of photos and upload them to your Zee Files. Then give me the password so I can see them."

"Nice try," Zee said. "We'll send you photos though. WhatsApp will work just fine."

The girls both settled into their beds and turned off the lights. Zee's mind, buzzing with anticipation for winter break, was ready for a deep restful sleep. She slid underneath the covers, put her headphones on, and pulled the sheet up close around her neck. The meditation music started to play. She closed her eyes and her head sunk into her pillow. For the first time at The Hollows, her bed actually felt comfortable.

California, here we come, she repeated to herself as she fell asleep.

THE END

Read on to see what happens with Zee and her friends in Book 4 of The Zee Files, *A Very Malibu Holiday.*

1
READY TO GO

This is our last breakfast in London!" Mackenzie "Zee" Blue Carmichael squealed as she skipped into the kitchen. The night before, Zee had arrived back at home in Notting Hill from The Hollows Creative Arts Academy, the private boarding school in the Costwolds where Zee had just finished her first semester.

"Last breakfast, Zee?" Zee's dad asked her.

"Well, not the last one *ever*, Dad," Zee said. "But for, like, a very long time!"

"Two weeks, Zee. We'll be gone for two weeks. I hope you didn't pack up your entire room. We just moved in a few months ago."

The Carmichaels—Zee, her mom, dad, and twin siblings Phoebe and Connor—had finally settled into their new home after moving to London from California in the fall for Mr. Carmichael's new job. But for the winter holiday break they were heading back to California, where Zee would see her friends from her old school, Brookdale Academy, and be able to visit her favorite places to eat, play, and be merry.

Zee couldn't wait to get to Malibu, where Mrs. Carmichael rented a house for their vacation. Zee had already made plans for a sleepover with her best friend Chloe Lawrence-Johnson, who still went to Brookdale. Even better, Zee's other Brookdale BFF Ally Stern was also returning to California. Ally's family had moved to Paris a few years ago when her dad took a job at the *Financial Times*. But recently her parents separated, and this year Ally was spending the holidays with her mom in California. With all three friends finally back together, Zee had big plans for a fun-filled reunion in Malibu.

"What time is our flight?" Zee said, sitting down at the kitchen table and excitedly digging into her eggs and toast.

"Not until this evening," Mr. Carmichael said just as his phone rang. "But if we're ready to go by noon, we should make good time."

Mr. Carmichael stood up to take the call in the other room, leaving Zee to eat breakfast and daydream about her plans in Malibu. She turned to her mother at the counter. "While we're home, let's do all of the holiday things! We can do a bunch of shopping and see all of the holiday decorations, and we can get cookies and those crazy good hot chocolates from the mall, and watch all of the Christmas movies and parades! And then we can take the twins to go see Santa!" Zee rambled. "I'm so excited to get back home. Oh, and Chloe! She has to come visit. Like soon. Like, *immediately*! And then Ally is supposed to come and see me! This will be the best. Holiday. EVER!"

"Yes indeed," Mrs. Carmichael said. "And I have big plans too! I'm going to be vlogging the entire vacation, from day to night. I have to keep creating content, you know." Mrs. Carmichael had recently become a social media influencer, thanks to her Instagram @twobycarmichael. She'd earned more than 15,000 followers from posting photos of her life as a mom of young twins, and the number of likes on her content has only grown since the family's move to London. Apparently, people liked seeing fashionable moms with their kids at places like Buckingham Palace and Harrod's.

"And of course, we have to bake cookies, and take photos of the twins in matching holiday outfits, and decorate the house," Mrs. Carmichael added. "I may need more than one tree. And... ooh, a party. We should have a party. We need. To have. A party!"

Zee rolled her eyes towards the ceiling. *Can't we just hang at the beach and have some chill time that won't be all over Instagram?* she thought. Though she liked that her mother was in the festive mood and that she was savvy at social media, Zee was annoyed at how her mother has become so obsessed with how things looked in pictures. Back in Brookdale, Mrs. Carmichael was more into gardening and crafts. Now she barely got her hands dirty.

Zee looked at her mother. "Yeah, could be fun. But Mom, do you think you'll be able to handle all that?"

"Of course! Between having Camilla and you to help, we'll be fine! And don't forget, your brother Adam is going to meet us in Malibu the day after we arrive." Camilla was the twins' nanny and had been taking care of them a lot while Zee was at The Hollows.

"Cool! A full house once again," Zee said. *But what about these parties she's talking about? Am I ever going to have a moment alone with my own mother? Or my friends?*

Zee took her phone out and texted Ally, excited to touch base with her friend before she hopped on her flight.

Zee

> Ally!!! Ally in Cali! Could there be anything better?!

A few moments went by before Ally responded:

Ally

> Hi! My aunt's picking me up at the airport tonight I'll be at her place for most of the time.

Zee

> So when do you think you could come to the house?

Ally

> I don't know. I have to see when I get there.

Zee was slightly disappointed but hopeful.

Zee

> Okay, well, we will be there the entire time and I will have your bed ready, hahahhaha!!

Ally

> Yes! Best holiday ever! Or at least better than last year!

Zee

> Yes! Where's your mom, by the way?

Ally

> She's already in Cali. She'll be at my aunt's house, I assume.

Zee

> Okay!!! Can't wait to seeeee you...

• • •

Zee got up from the kitchen table and went to her room to pack the last of her things. She had spent very little time in her own bedroom in her London house, since she lived at The Hollows boarding school full time. But Notting Hill was starting to feel more like home.

Her room now had one thing to make it even more comforting: a valued piece that had recently arrived in the mail after many months—her treasured acoustic guitar. The movers had forgotten to put it in the truck when the Carmichaels left California, so they had mailed it off to London months ago. But thanks to cargo shipping, it took forever to get to Notting Hill. Zee smiled when she spotted the guitar waiting for her in the corner of the room, sitting upright on its stand. "There you are!" she exclaimed. "Come to mama!"

Zee played a few chords on the instrument, humming along to the song she'd recently written for The Hollows Creative Arts Festival, where Zee had performed a solo. She couldn't wait to bring the guitar back to campus back and jam on it in her dorm room. Her roommate, Jameela Chopra, was usually gone at ballet practice after school anyway, so Zee thought she could squeeze in some guitar practice while Jameela was out.

Zee thought about how she wanted to create new songs with her pal Jasper Chapman, who produced music and was her best guy friend at The Hollows. And she thought about the guy who had helped her put together the melody for the song she performed, and with whom she had a brief but complex relationship with: Archie Saint John, a ridiculously good-looking and talented guitarist for a year nine student. He had taken a quick liking to Zee and the two became fast friends, and eventually boyfriend and girlfriend, which meant they had hung out together. A lot. Archie had liked hanging around Zee so much, too much, that she quickly felt smothered and broke things off with him. They were just friends now. *And that's a good place for us to be,* Zee thought to herself.

For now, it was time to head to California, back to her old stomping grounds and far from Archie Saint John. She put the guitar back down on its stand and finished packing up the last of her things.

Acknowledgments

Thank you to the team at Target, Christina Hennington, Ann Maranzano, and Kate Udvari. You really make this the dream.

To my West Margin Press family, Jennifer Newens, Rachel Metzger, Olivia Ngai, and Angie Zbornik. Thank you for your dedication to this series.

To Andre Des Rochers, Bejide Davis, and the entire Granderson Des Rochers team, thank you for always representing me well.

Stephanie Smith, you are the best collaborator and friend. It's really an honor and such a pleasure to create these books with you.

To my family and friends, thank you for all of your support; it means everything.

To my readers, thank you always. It's really the honor of my life to write for you.

MORE ZEE!

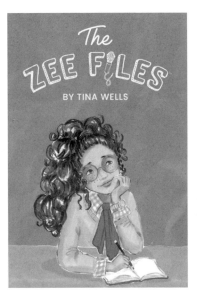